BUZZBUGS

BUZZBUGS

BRUCE CARTER

F- Car

79

FREDERICK WARNE

New York • London

For Harry, 1963–76

Frederick Warne & Co., Inc.
New York, New York

Manufactured in the U.S.A.
LCC: 77-075044
ISBN: 0-7232-6148-2

1 2 3 4 5 6 7 8 9 10

AUTHOR'S NOTE

My thanks are due to the South African Tourist Board which, with great knowledge and consideration, took me to the magnificent Kalahari-Gemsbok National Park in northwest Cape Province. My experiences there, under exceptionally stormy conditions, formed the background for a part of this book.

This is, however, a work of imaginative fiction, in which the other localities and all the characters are fictitious. The entomological details are also imaginary.

March 1976   BRUCE CARTER

Millbeck, a village in northwest England, was occupied long ago by the Norsemen who left their mark on the English language spoken in that region to this day. So as you read *Buzzbugs* you will come across several unusual words. For example, *beck*— a creek; *ghyll*—a small beck or stream; *rowan*—a tree; *vole*—a field mouse; *shippon*—a cattle barn; *fell* and *fellside*—hill and hillside; *offcomer*—stranger; *knacker*—one who buys worn-out horses for slaughter to use as animal food; *spinney*—small woods with undergrowth; *scree*—a bunch of small loose stones on a slope.

PART ONE

Several events led to the buzzbug tragedy at Mill-beck that summer. The first happened in the village, and was a bad omen by any reckoning.

John was in his workshop in the hayloft of the barn. He was working on an old generator, an essential component of his hydroelectric scheme. John was confident that he could make his father's milking machine independent of the expensive main electricity, and perhaps the whole house, too. That would save them about £200 a year, a large sum of money for anyone as poor as the Thomsons.

"Don't you see, Dad? There's power in the beck. That water's just going to waste. I'm going to tap the power and convert it into electricity. The world's full of power going to waste while we pinch all the coal and oil and . . ."

His father had not really understood. It all seemed a long way from hill farming in Cumbria.

His mother had said, "Eh, young John, wash that grease off your hands—time for tea."

John did not worry. He just got on with the job.

The next day he intended to begin laying the cable, slinging it from tree to tree. It was going to work all right. There was no reason why it shouldn't. But how he longed to switch on for the first time!

He had just put his tools away for the day when he heard the sound of a car draw up in the yard below. It did so violently, halting in a long skid, scattering the chickens.

John looked out through the hayloft's loading bay, and his heart sank. The car was Mrs. Effingham's, a mud-spattered mauve Jensen convertible. She only came to the Thomson farm when there was trouble. John watched in dismay as Mrs. Effingham got out and knocked loudly on the door with her hunting crop.

John's father opened the door. John could imagine his feelings when he recognized the stout frame of Mrs. Effingham in her jodhpurs and tweed jacket.

There was no greeting. Mrs. Effingham went straight into the attack.

"Mr. Thomson, I am a patient woman, but your sheep are on my land again. Twelve of them. I am legally permitted to demand a pound a head for the loss of grazing—a pound a head a day—and this time I shall do so."

She scarcely paused to catch her breath. "Moreover, they knocked down a six-yard length of wall getting into my field. That must be repaired without delay. It is one of my best fields, and I have had to take my brood mares out of it."

John heard his father begin to apologize and be

cut short. "It's not enough to say you're sorry. It's sorry, sorry, sorry all the time from you. You're a bad neighbor, Mr. Thomson, and a bad, lazy farmer."

John felt the blood rise to his face, and his hands gripped the stone of the wall beside him. One day, he felt sure, he would attack that woman. He could kill her—he really could—for insulting his father and making their lives a misery. Tears of rage formed in his eyes. "I can't bear it any longer," he told himself in despair. "I can't bear it."

Through his half-closed eyes he saw mistily over the gate and stone wall his father's fields, rich meadows but small in contrast with Mrs. Effingham's which almost surrounded the Thomson farm. Her land stretched as far as the eye could see on the other side of the beck, the other side of the valley, laid out as if seen obliquely from a low-flying plane.

Mrs. Effingham was getting back into her car. John watched her start it up just below him and, with her hard, authoritative hands on the steering wheel, back the big, open car furiously out of the yard. From where he stood he could have dropped a rock onto her head.

Instead, he drew back inside the barn and closed his ears to the sound of the powerful Jensen, tires squealing, racing away up the village, threatening death at every bend in the road.

How could she? How could she be so cruel and arrogant and ruthless? How could she, so ugly, live in a village that was so peaceful and lovely, and so

9

full of nice, kind, humble people, like his own father and mother?

Twelve pounds! That was a terrible lot of money for a poor hill farmer to find. The sheep in the valley were always wandering from field to field. Everyone knew that you cannot keep them in— except Mrs. Effingham, the one woman, with her stud of thoroughbred horses and a thousand acres of best grazing land, who could afford the loss of a few mouthfuls of grass. John swept up some of the electrical cord from the floor and put the generator away on a shelf. (He had found it on the Barrow rubbish heap and had renovated it and rewound the wiring over the past weeks. It worked like a dream.)

Tea was a silent and depressing meal. John's father, who was usually so cheerful and light-hearted and full of chatter, hardly said a word and hardly ate a thing. "He's near the end of his tether," John told himself. "He knows that woman's trying to drive us out so that she can buy up our farm with its two best rich fields slap in the middle of her land like islands. Our farm. Gartholme Farm. Belonged to Thomsons since 1600 and before then. And that greedy offcomer's determined to get our one hundred acres. I wouldn't put it past her to drive our sheep over the walls into her own fields. Then she comes around here in her expensive car and insults my father. My father, who never did an unkind thing to anyone in his life."

The ham almost stuck in John's throat, and it was their own cured ham, like butter in your mouth.

The gray mist of rage still half blinded him when he excused himself and got up from the table in their flagstoned kitchen.

His mother's hens were on the porch seats. They had been there most of the day, sheltering from the heat. Now the sun was low across the valley. What a summer! The hottest anyone could remember. Many of the ghylls had dried up. The water was low in their tank, sunk deep in the orchard above their house—sunk there in 1676 according to the engraved stone below the overflow. But there was still enough water in the beck for John's hydroelectric scheme.

But John's plans were for once lost in the back of his mind. All he could think about for the present was Mrs. Effingham and his father's predicament.

Slowly, as John sat there, a plan formed in his mind. Even while he talked to his collie, Scot, and addressed his mother's hens by name when they hopped about him, the plan of counterattack developed.

When John got up and walked slowly across the dusty yard, the sun had gone down behind Craig Fell, although it would spread its bright rays across the other side of the valley for another hour, changing the color of bracken, grass, rowan trees, and stone walls minute by minute.

John was well aware of the wrongness of what he was about to do. He had never done anything illegal and destructively violent in his life. He regretted that he had to do what he was going to

11

do. But he also knew that, unless something was done, Mrs. Effingham's cruel harassment would go on and on until his father cracked. And then Gartholme Farm would be swallowed up by that woman's insatiable appetite. Only counterharassment could save them. That was John's calculation.

It was not dark until eleven o'clock. His father and mother were watching the late-night news on television—on the set the shop's manager had given John because he said it was unrepairable. John had thought otherwise.

John let himself out through the back door. Scot whined his disappointment at being left behind. But only for a moment. Scot was a wise, good dog, full of tact.

John collected the two screwdrivers and the big steel curved lever, like a burglar's jimmy, that his father used for home-smithy work sometimes, and set off across the fields. He climbed the stone walls at the places which he knew, from long boyhood experience, were easiest.

The third mare paddock would be the best. He guessed that it was to this field Mrs. Effingham would have had the best brood mares moved—every unborn foal worth many thousands of pounds.

There were owls in the oaks above Tithe Farm. One of them flapped down ahead, toward the beck. John caught glimpses of the big body, solid black against the velvet ultramarine of the starlit sky, and heard it, seconds later, calling from the trees ahead as if beckoning him on. John felt that he knew all the owls—the four tawnys in Shag Wood, the two barn owls down at Slitherlack, and the rest—as he knew every yard and every stone of his route.

He crossed the busy, white-flecked beck by the stepping-stones, vaulted the stile into the next field, and five minutes later was in forbidden territory, cautiously approaching a gate.

One beam from his flashlight showed him that his journey had been wasted, that fate had been up to one of its ironical jokes. For the gate was already open. Not only was it open, but it had been forced open violently with the same sort of tools that he had brought with him to commit the offense that had already been committed. The oak gate, painted deep blue, had been attacked by someone who felt as desperately antagonistic toward Mrs. Effingham as he did. The staple and padlock which had secured the gate to the solid oak post had been wrenched out, and the gate had swung open.

All but one of the brood mares had already gained their freedom, and as John stood there, contemplating the vandalism he himself had planned, the last of the mares approached out of the darkness and sniffed perfunctorily at the post. John heard her breathing, then saw her bulk in the dim light. She was taking slow, tentative steps toward the unusual opportunity that suddenly presented itself. She paused, staring curiously at the open space that led to freedom, and then walked through in the tracks of the others who had gone before.

She trotted heavily up the lane, her unshod hoofs

clip-clopping softly on the tarmac, like a distant Indian's tom-tom beat of victory.

Thanks to some anonymous ally, by dawn the Effingham mares would be spread over the length and breadth of the valley and, with luck, far beyond toward Grange and Barrow and Workington.

John was home in half the time it had taken him to reach his destination. He replaced the tools carefully, spoke to Scot briefly to say good night and silence his soft whines of welcome, and crept into his bedroom.

He did not fall asleep for at least an hour. The question that was to nag at him for weeks was already worrying away at his conscience, like a terrier at a rat hole. He meant to do it, he would have done it, and it had been done. Was he not as guilty as if he had torn off that staple and padlock?

Then, insidiously, a sly voice intervened—"But you *didn't* do it. *You* didn't."

Lucy said, "Poor Balliol—you need rich, crisp grass in August. Not this burned-up rubbish."

Lucy Appleby lay in the sun, dressed in shorts and shirt, looking straight up into Balliol's nostrils. The old gelding appeared to be taking the shortage of grazing philosophically, and tore at the brown grass with the same abstracted air as if it were what his mistress wanted for him—rich, crisp, young grass.

Sometimes Balliol paused in his munching and looked up with old black eyes at the horizon of rolling fells or at Lucy's face just below him. When Balliol looked at her, Lucy liked to pretend that all sorts of loyal deep thoughts were passing through the pony's mind.

"I am going to take you into the orchard," said Lucy decisively. "You need the nourishment of some meadow foxtail, crested dogstail, and sweet vernal—to spare you the Latin names. Plenty in the orchard."

Lucy clipped the leading rein into Balliol's halter ring. "Come on, silly, a feast fit for a king."

Balliol appeared as unmoved by her plea as he was unmoved by her pull on the leading rein. He was sticking it out with the dried-up grass of his own familiar field.

"You're a fool!" Lucy exclaimed crossly. She'd had no idea when, at the age of about six, she had named her pony Balliol that it was the name of a brainy Oxford college. She just thought it sounded nice. After she was told, she interpreted her choice as a presentiment. Of course Balliol was brainy. The cleverest pony in the north of England.

And now he was being a fool.

He came at last, allowing his head to be pulled up, but taking a last bite of brown rubbish on the way. Lucy led him off. It was a firm, stately progress across the field, except when Lucy walked barefoot on a thistle. She said "ouch" loudly and sat down for a moment to pull out the prickles.

Balliol took the opportunity to grab several mouthfuls of the short burned-up grass as if storing for a famine.

15

Lucy had no mother, and a father who was a botanist. She did not know what a mother was, except that her friends like Jane Ensome, Mary Caldecott, and John Thomson had mothers. Her own mother, she had been told long ago, had died at her birth.

Lucy's father was a doctor of science—Dr. Stuart Appleby. She loved him dearly and did not see him as often as she would have liked because he spent his weekdays at North Manchester in the university, and was at home only from Friday afternoons until Monday mornings. Sometimes he was away for longer periods on field research. He had recently returned from three weeks in Africa.

Lucy's nearest thing to a mother was Rachel— Rachel Deering, a plump, kind, simple woman of thirty-five who had not married and for whom Lucy was the nearest thing to a daughter she was ever likely to have. Rachel lived at End House when Lucy's father was away, and at her house in the village when he came back.

Unlike John Thomson, Lucy had no particular problems. She enjoyed life at End House and at Rangarth School a bus ride away. Her main interests in life were Balliol and birds.

Lucy was a keen ornithologist and a member of the National Society for the Protection of Birds. She was known in the village for her knowledge of bird lore, and for always carrying with her wherever she went a pair of binoculars in a battered case. She had also attained temporary fame for her prize-winning entry in the model competition in the village fete—a marvelous and huge papier-mâché golden eagle.

Lucy's idea of a perfect afternoon was to ride off into the fells on Balliol with some food, and of course her field glasses, looking for buzzards, peregrine falcons, and above all, the pair of golden eagles that nested not far from Millbeck. Large birds of prey were what Lucy liked most.

She untied the string that held shut the orchard gate and pushed it open. "Here, Balliol, riches beyond the dreams of avarice." She led him in, and before she could shut the date, the pony's head was down and he was tearing away at the long, rich grass.

The sloping orchard was watered above by a spring which never dried up, even in a drought as bad as this one. Years ago, Dr. Appleby used to have the Thomson sheep in once a year for a few days to keep the grass down, but he had now planted so many rare plants and shrubs and roses among the fruit trees that it had become impractical to protect them all. So the grass had now been allowed to grow wild, the home of countless voles and mice, to Lucy's satisfaction.

Strictly speaking, Balliol had no business to be in the orchard at all, which was now forbidden to livestock. But Lucy considered, reasonably enough, that if she held Balliol's leading rein and guided him with care, no harm could be done to the plants and great benefit could be done to Balliol's stomach—which Lucy was certain was three-quarters empty, although anyone else would judge it to be four-quarters full.

For some time this arrangement worked well. Balliol tore at the virgin grass, moving forward and sideways unpredictably and without plan, as grazing animals do, only restrained by Lucy from going too near the plants, which Dr. Appleby had planted in small scattered beds cut out of the grass. Once or twice Balliol threw up his head and dragged an apple from a low branch, munching noisily with his old worn-down teeth.

Sometimes Lucy lay in the grass beside the pony, listening to the swish of his tail and the shrill, mournful cry of the buzzards from Rhyllwood. She caught sight of the birds circling above the beck high up the valley. For a long time the sky remained cloudless and clear of all but the playing buzzards, and deep blue as it had been for days past. Then she caught sight of the corner of a black cloud, still far to the west and over the sea. It grew larger as she watched it, and she felt the first cool brush of a damp breeze on her cheeks.

Balliol had finished with this corner of the orchard. Lucy got up and led him between two William trees, picking a pear for herself on the way, and making for a clear patch of grass near the stone wall at the top of the orchard. The first faint rumble sounded over the fells, and Balliol suddenly threw up his head and stood stock still.

"Come on, silly, it's only a bit of thunder," Lucy said coaxingly. "You don't mind thunder. Not all that much, anyway."

It was true that Balliol—solid, untemperamental Balliol—did not react violently to thunder as some ponies do, even if he did not much care for it. But when another clap sounded he began to shiver, his head went up again, and Lucy saw that his eyes were wide with fear.

She decided to wait for a minute or two, hoping there would be no more thunder, before trying again to move the pony. But then she began to fear what would happen if the pony shied violently, broke free, and ran amok in the orchard with all its precious plants. She began to regret that she had brought him in at all.

The breeze had got up and had become a wind, a gentle wind still, but carrying with it the first touch of cool air they had felt for days. Yet Balliol was sweating as if just returned from a long hard ride. Lucy looked at him anxiously and saw his head turn and then toss up again in fear.

Then Lucy realized that it was not what he had heard with his sharp ears that had terrified her pony, but what he had seen with his black eyes. Two yards in front of Balliol's forelegs there protruded from the long grass, like a spent shell that has failed to explode, a dark cylindrical object. At first sight it did not look in the least alarming. But its strangeness increased in proportion with the length of time she studied it.

Then she began to feel afraid. Not terror-struck like Balliol. But afraid.

"It is no good just looking—from this distance anyway," Lucy told herself firmly. She had her fair share of common sense and had learned to be independent, which made her less timorous than some twelve-year-olds.

Holding tight to the end of the leading rein, she stepped forward and bent down over the object. It was about a yard long and eight inches in diameter, grayish brown in color like the soil around it from which it looked as if it had emerged—although that was a ridiculous idea, Lucy told herself. Its surface looked rough and was clearly scaled in lateral segments. Most curious of all, at the tapered, upper end, there projected a rubber-ball-shaped extension with a further, softer looking extension above it, while just below, there was a single short stump. In poor light, or in a nightmare, the whole object might have been mistaken for an Egyptian mummy in miniature, a mummy whose wrappings had begun to fall apart with age, revealing the head and the remains of one of its arms.

As Lucy bent over it she began to feel a cold flush creep over her, and she suddenly understood for the first time what it was that had caused her pony to be seized with fear. There was something not *right* about the thing. It was not right in shape, in color, or in its position. It had no business to be shaped as it was shaped, to have that sort of head with what looked like a sort of jaunty feather sticking out of it, or to give the impression that it had either just emerged from the earth or been thrust violently into it.

If her father, as a scientist, had not instilled in Lucy a sense of curiousity, she would have withdrawn at this point. Instead, and now thoroughly frightened, she forced herself to put out her hand toward it. She did not touch it. She had the palm of her hand close above the surface of the object and was about to put her hand on it when it moved. The movement was scarcely perceptible, but it was a movement. There was no doubt of it, though it was perhaps more a response, a shrinking back, than a positive movement.

Lucy withdrew her hand and was at once so frightened and so puzzled that she put it close again, closer than before and watching even more carefully.

This time the thing gave a noticeable twitch, as if it were alive and alarmed, the scales enlarging or diminishing in size according to the direction of the flexing. And the head twisted, as if searching sightlessly for some antagonist.

Balliol saw the movement this time. He saw it with those scared black eyes as clearly as Lucy saw it. And they both responded to their fear in the same way, Lucy flinching back and the pony shying, jerking back his head and dragging Lucy with him.

In the same second, like a fateful final chord to this overture of fear, a tremendous clap of thunder sounded overhead. This was altogether too much for Balliol, who reared again, dragging the leading rein from Lucy's grasp, and galloped off, sending clods of earth and grass from his flying hooves high into the air.

To Lucy's relief, he made straight for the open gate to his field and was soon far from sight over the ridge. Lucy ran in his tracks as far as the gate, slamming it shut and tying it, and then leaned against it in relief and exhaustion.

She did not go back to the thing in the grass. She was prepared to examine it again but only with someone else to share her findings. Her father would not be back until the evening. She did not want to upset Rachel, who was easily frightened. But John would do. He was scientific and curious and unafraid.

Normally Lucy rode Balliol up to Gartholme Farm to see John. But the pony was still in an uneasy state when she ran to the far end of the field to retrieve his leading rein. No, today she would have to use her old bicycle.

She got it out of the shippon and rode up through the village, waving to people she knew as she passed them. The black clouds almost filled the sky, frequent claps of thunder echoed about the fells, the Thomson cows were settling themselves down to wait for the rain, and the ducks were swaggering with pleasure. It was rather like what Lucy imagined it to be in the East just before the monsoon broke, with the parched land and its inhabitants eagerly awaiting the downpour.

The first drops of rain fell as great blobs in the dust as Lucy reached the Thomson farmyard. She left her bicycle on the porch, apologizing to the hens for the disturbance, and walked straight in through the big old oak front door. Gartholme was a second home to her, and the Thomsons regarded her as one of the family.

"Well, Lucy love, it's what we all need," Mrs. Thomson greeted her. And, as yet another clap of thunder crashed overhead, she added, "Though I don't see why there has to be such a noise about it." She offered Lucy tea and told her John was in the barn.

Lucy found him in his usual position, bent over his workbench with Scot at his feet. John turned and grinned when she came in, and the dog strolled toward her, brushing the air with his black-and-white tail.

"You've got to come. There's something really funny in the orchard," Lucy said breathlessly.

"What sort of funny?" John asked, unimpressed and, so far, uninterested.

"Something going into the ground. Or coming out of it. I don't know which."

John was back at work with a small screwdriver. "You mean an earthworm?"

"Don't be silly," said Lucy impatiently. She thought she could rely on John to take her seriously. She would have to be patient. So she sat down on the wooden floor and, while she stroked Scot behind his ear, recounted what she had seen and Balliol's reaction to it.

When she had finished, John put down his tools again and turned around. He was the same age as Lucy but shorter—a chunky boy you could call him, with serious gray eyes and a touch of ginger in his hair, like his mother. He regarded Lucy more as a friendly sister than as a friend, and he respected her specialized knowledge of birds and flowers and plants. He knew she wasn't joking now, though he could not believe all that she had told him.

"I think you must have imagined it moved," he said. "Easy enough. I expect you'd been dreaming in the heat, like Alice before she saw the rabbit in the white gloves."

"Well, you just come and *see,* then," said Lucy indignantly. "It moved all right—sort of twitched. And Balliol saw it too. You can't fool a pony. They can't imagine things. You just come and see," she repeated.

They went over to the loading bay and looked out. The storm was at its height, the rain falling in sheets, the thunder rolling almost continuously, and the lightning flashing over the fellsides, illuminating whipped rowans and sycamores bending before the sudden gusts of wind. A muddy stream had already formed in the yard, racing down toward the gate into the field below. The ducks were walking up and down in it, spreading their wings to the rain. A fresh smell of clean wetness was driven into the barn on the wind.

"Not in this, thanks," said John.

"Coward."

But when it began to ease off later, it was John who suggested that they should go. He got out his bicycle, as old as Lucy's but beautifully cared for, and they pedaled off through the village. The ghylls that ran under the road were already flowing fast,

24

adding to the feeling that life was starting up again after the weeks of hot lethargy.

Rachel was at the door of End House, in her apron and with her arms akimbo like a drawing of a farmer's stout wife from a fairy tale. She was used to Lucy's coming and going and knew that she was too sensible to do anything silly or worrying.

"Dinner's ready in ten minutes, love," she said. "Hullo, young John. How's your mum and dad?"

Lucy said, "Shan't be long." She put her bicycle in the shippon and led John up the path to the orchard. The storm had turned the path into a little ghyll, and they took off their shoes and walked barefoot when they reached the glistening, dripping grass. On the steep slope, and under the pressure of the downpour, the soil from some of Dr. Appleby's beds had eroded onto the grass, staining it gray-brown. It was as if a giant bucket of water had been sloshed over the valleyside.

Lucy knew every inch of the orchard and had no difficulty in finding the exact spot, close to the wall, where she had been standing with Balliol. But the storm had brought about many small changes. The stone wall now glistened, when an hour before, the rocks had been dull gray and the little hart's-tongue ferns growing between the rocks had been flattened. The wind and rain had also beaten the grass flat, obscuring even Balliol's hoof marks.

Lucy squatted down and searched for the object. This was the exact spot, she was in no doubt of that. But there was no sign of it. She lifted the sodden grass and felt about with her hands.

"You said it was sticking up out of the ground," said John. "You ought to be able to see it better with the grass all flat like that."

Lucy ignored him and began pulling out handfuls of grass angrily. "I tell you it was here," she repeated after a few minutes. "Look, you see this soil?" She pointed at a small patch that might have been exposed by her scrabbling. Or it might have marked the spot from which the object had protruded. "This is where it was. Really it was."

"It looks as if he's gone home again," said John laconically. "Perhaps he decided he didn't like our climate." He sauntered off back to his shoes, and a minute later was pedaling away in the last of the rain—no more than a light drizzle now—back up the hill, back to midday dinner, and back to his anxieties. "When will the police come?" was the question that dominated John's mind, not "What was the mysterious object Lucy found?"

Lucy watched him go, feeling half frightened and half angry. That strange moment, lasting no more than a minute, the fear she had shared with her pony, the thing responding to the proximity of her hand, the sudden movement as if she had stirred life into it—could she really have dreamed it all? She had to admit that there was no shred of evidence left to confirm that it had really happened, even that she had brought Balliol out of his field to graze in the orchard.

The gate was tied up, as it had been before. His leading rein was hanging on the peg in the shippon, as it had been before. All other evidence had been washed away. And all that was left was the memory of that faintly stirring cylindrical thing nestling in the grass, just here.

When she had been about eight, Lucy had prayed aloud one evening in bed that Balliol could talk. Earlier on that day she had seen a heron, loping low overhead, quite unafraid of them. She had said, "Look at that heron, Balliol!" She had so much wanted him to understand and to say, "Oh, that's a heron, is it?"

Even then, at eight, she knew the idea was ridiculous. But four years later, as she answered Rachel's summons to dinner and made her way barefoot through the soaking grass, she thought ruefully of the strangeness of life that only she and an aged pony shared the secret of seeing that moving, brown-gray object, and shared their fear of it.

The police came, as John knew that they would. The black car with the blue light on its roof pulled into the Gartholme farmyard at tea time, a plain-clothes officer sitting alongside the uniformed driver. His father arrived back from walling over at Mrs. Effingham's, a job that he said wearily would take four days.

John watched from the barn as the plainclothes detective got out and began to talk to his father. They were almost out of earshot, but Mr. Thomson spoke louder, so John could not hear the questions but could hear the answers his father gave.

"Oh, aye, I've heard. A terrible business. . . . No, I've seen nowt—walling all day. Took my dinner and got caught in t'storm. . . . Oh, aye, we've had our little disagreements. Nothing serious, though."

Then they went inside, and Mr. Thomson came and called out to John. He made his way slowly down the barn steps and out into the yard, feeling sick with apprehension. In the kitchen it all looked very informal and friendly. Too friendly, thought John, remembering all those casual interrogations he had seen on television. Both policemen were sipping big cups of strong tea, and his mother was laughing at something one of them had said. His father was taking off his boots in the corner.

To John's astonishment, both policemen got up when they saw him, and the uniformed one (John remembered having once seen him directing the traffic in Barrow) drew up a chair for him.

"I expect you've heard the news about the horses?" the detective said. John shook his head while he searched his conscience. He knew that they had escaped, but what other news was there? "Mrs. Effingham lost all her brood mares last night. They got out somehow," continued the detective.

In a sudden moment of panic, on hearing the word "somehow," John had a vision of Mrs. Effingham's head groom discovering the open gate and, fearing he might be blamed, securing it again and knocking down some more stone wall to account for the mass escape—common wall between Thomson and Effingham land. Then his father would bear the responsibility for the loss. And that could mean bankruptcy and selling out.

The detective did not appear to notice John's sudden tension and the fear in his eyes. He continued, in a kind, matter-of-fact voice, "We're calling on everyone in the village asking them to keep a lookout for these mares—especially keen-eyed young lads like you who're always moving about."

He sipped the tea approvingly and said, "You make a nice pot, Mrs. Thomson." Then, talking to them all, "The trouble is that this storm has probably panicked some of them. What with being in a strange place and all. We've already heard of one not far from Coniston, nearly run into in the heavy rain. And we think there's another nearly twenty miles away, up in the fells."

John wondered if he dared to ask the question. Then, when there was a pause in the conversation, he plucked up his courage. When he spoke, his voice did not sound like his own. "How did they get out, sir?"

"Oh, through the gate," said the detective.

"But they're always padlocked, aren't they?" said Mr. Thomson.

"Aye, but some vandal broke the locks." He got up from the table and picked up the raincoat from the back of the chair where he had slung it.

"There's a lot of money in bloodstock, and where there's money there's usually trouble. And bad blood, if you'll forgive my little joke. I expect there're enemies among these bloodstock breeders."

He moved toward the door, and Mr. Thomson opened it for him. "Well, yours is the last house in the village, but we'd best get back for the latest reports."

When they had gone, Mrs. Thomson, who never minced her words, said, "Well, that'll teach that terrible woman to complain about a few wandering sheep. 'Whatsoever a man soweth, that shall he also reap.' And that goes for women, too." She turned to her husband. "Now mind, if any of those wretched nags are found on *our* land, you're to charge five pounds a head for loss of grazing."

John's relief was short-lived. The police returned the next morning, this time to talk to him alone, with his parents' permission. He sat in their big black car, which smelled of old leather and cigarettes. They did not drive him anywhere. They just stayed in the yard, which struck John as odd. A car was for going in.

It was the same detective, and he was very polite and kind. They sat side by side in the back, and he said, "We just wanted to have a quick word with you, if you don't mind, about that gate business over at your neighbors'. Some of the mares are still missing and others are likely to abort, so it's been quite an expensive and serious business.

"Now, we know that your father and Mrs. Effingham are not on the best of terms owing to difficulties which sometimes crop up in the country. You know how it is," he went on, very man-to-man. "Now, you're a good, loyal, loving son, I've no doubt, and it did just cross our minds . . ."

Afterward, John thought he had stood up to the questioning rather well. He had not criticized Mrs. Effingham in any way and had suggested noninterest in what the detectives called "the difficulties" between his father and their neighbor. He tried to give the impression that he was so bound up in his work that he did not really take much interest in what was happening in the world outside.

But John also knew that he remained a suspect, that they would probably be back for another questioning, hoping to crack his story of going to bed and getting up at the usual time. And the thought that he might have left some clue somewhere on that night prowl—a clue that perhaps they had already found—continued to nag the back of his mind.

The next morning, his father sent him into Rangarth to get some syringes of Mylodol from the vet. John found himself looking suspiciously from left to right as he cycled through the town. When he saw a policeman strolling along the pavement, he nearly turned off down a side road to avoid being seen.

For the first time, John knew what it was like to have a bad conscience. And for the first time he knew a little of what it must be like to be a real criminal, never at ease with yourself or the world about you.

The third event linked with the Millbeck tragedy that summer occurred more than five thousand miles away and in a temperature close to 100° F. Dr. Appleby's three-week-long trip to Africa had taken him to the Kalahari desert in northwest Cape Province in the Republic of South Africa. This is a vast area of rolling sand dunes, dry river beds, and scrub, once populated by fierce bushmen.

Nowadays, except for one or two isolated settlements and camps for adventurous scientists and tourists, its inhabitants are roaming herds of springbok, gemsbok, hartebeest, wildebeest and other ungulates, the predatory leopard and cheetah and lion, and the scavenging hyena.

When no rain has fallen for months, the Kalahari can present a parched and stark appearance. Even the toughest thorn bushes appear lifeless, and the animals search listlessly for a shred of dry grass, their rib cages making them look like walking X rays of themselves. During these times, only the eagles and falcons and the slowly circling vultures appear content with life.

But a light shower of rain sweeping across these hundreds of square miles can transform the scene overnight. A green mist of grass tempers the harsh gold and brown of the sand, and a multitude of flowers colors the dunes. A naturalist's dream at any time, after a touch of rain the Kalahari becomes a paradise for botanists. For the student of the rarer species of succulents, this desert has a special interest. And Dr. Appleby was a world authority on this form of plant life which, like the camel of the desert, can live for so long on its own liquid resources.

Dr. Appleby reached Upington, the town in Cape Province nearest to the desert, early in August. He was met at the airport by an Afrikaaner naturalist, experienced in the Kalahari, named Piet Ackburg. Dr. Appleby took to him at once. He was a warmhearted young man, enthusiastic, and determined that the Englishman's mission should be successful.

They met the third member of their party in the lounge of a small hotel in Upington. A fan on the ceiling slowly stirred the hot air. From the bar across the hallway there came the sound of voices speaking in harsh Afrikaans. The decor was Dutch, a century ago. The beer was ice cold and unfamiliar. To Dr. Appleby, tired from his long journey, it all seemed very remote from the cool stone and old oak beams of End House, Millbeck.

"Please meet Mary Fleming, Dr. Appleby," said Mr. Ackburg in his slightly guttural voice.

Dr. Appleby got up as a young woman entered the room. She had a rather poor complexion, but was all smiles, and overweight—doing something about it—as she laughingly explained later. Dr. Appleby shook her hand warmly, studying her with interest at the same time, for he was about to spend two weeks with her and Mr. Ackburg in the desert and it was therefore important that they should all get on well together.

Mary Fleming had been recommended to Dr. Appleby by the head of the Department of Botany at the University of Northern Cape Town. She was completing what he described as an exceptional thesis on succulents and had traveled widely in the Kalahari on field research. She had never found the aucurula, the very rare branch of the genus *Rhipsalis* succulent, for which Dr. Appleby was searching. But she had a number of ideas where it might be found and, with Piet Ackburg as guide, was confident that their expedition would be a success.

Dr. Appleby went to bed that night feeling happy about his companions and excited at the prospect of their departure the following morning.

They set out in brilliant sunshine in their comprehensively equipped Land Rover and drove rapidly over dirt roads to the entrance to the Kalahari-Gemsbok National Park, a vast area of the desert open to adventurous tourists, where the flora and fauna are protected under natural conditions.

Dr. Appleby was awed by the harsh beauty of the desert and impressed by the seeming lack of fear among the animals. How Lucy would have loved to see the gay, leaping little springbok, so pretty in contrast to the dour wildebeest, the massive eland, and above all the great sleek lioness with her two cubs which they had followed for more than a mile across the dunes. Next time he determined to bring her with him, whatever the cost.

But above all it was the flowers that fascinated Dr. Appleby. He had never seen desert flowers in such profusion and such variety. Surely, if he was ever going to find the elusive little aucurula succulent, it would be here.

And he was right, although it was not until the ninth day of their expedition, when they were all tired from the heat which increased day by day, filthy from lack of washing, and weary of their limited variety of food and drink. All but three of their nights had been spent in the open, Mary in the Land Rover and the two men under canvas with a fire going all night to discourage predators, especially lions, and with the mournful cry of hyenas echoing across the dunes.

At first, Dr. Appleby had relished the rigors of their life together, and the excitement of discovering so many species of plant. By the end of the first week he was thankful for the goodwill of the other two, which kept his own spirits optimistic in spite of their many disappointments and anticlimaxes after they thought they were so close to their goal.

Throughout all the rigors they endured, Dr. Appleby's health remained good. He looked after it carefully, taking pills against sunburn and against intestinal disorders, too. He noticed that Mary Fleming was also taking pills, and their expedition was never delayed by sickness.

On their eighth night there was a tremendous

thunderstorm. Sheet and forked lightning flashed continuously over the desert horizons for hours on end, suddenly illuminating the camel-thorn trees and the startled faces of nearby gemsbok. At first the rain beat down on the tent as if reincarnated bushmen were hurling pellets at them. Then the volume became so great that they might have been at the base of a waterfall. When Dr. Appleby peered out at dawn he saw pools where it had seemed as if water had never lain since the Great Flood, and with the instant response that only the tropics can activate, already swarms of little midges and mosquitoes were dancing over the damp patches.

"I'm glad to see you weren't swept away," said Mary Fleming cheerfully as she emerged from the Land Rover and began to prepare breakfast. "To-day is the day for the aucurula, I feel it in my bones," she added optimistically.

As she had predicted, they found the precious little yellow succulent growing on the slopes of a dune, close to some blackthorn and not ten miles from the Botswana frontier.

Piet Ackburg, who had the eyes of a desert hawk, spotted the clump at a distance of almost half a mile. He did not say anything, but the other two noticed him suddenly swinging over the steering wheel and accelerating across the sand. Dr. Appleby saw it next, through his field glasses, and all he could exclaim was, "My God!"

They all piled out before the Land Rover had lurched back on its springs. Dr. Appleby knelt in

36

the damp sand beside the first plant as if he had reached the Holy Grail itself. Here it was at last! After all the planning, after all the traveling, the expense, discomfort, and heat—with the help of these two, he had reached his goal—a small leafless succulent with a modest but pretty little yellow flower. For Dr. Appleby, each petal might have been beaten out by nature from gold leaf.

After photographing the plants from every angle and confirming their exact position on the map, they began the delicate work of taking samples. Dr. Appleby, on behalf of North Manchester University, had been given authority by Pretoria to take up to 20 percent, but no more than one dozen, of any single group of the succulent. They were equipped with the tools, the pots, and plastic containers for the operation. But it was not easy, working in the loose sand, to avoid disturbing the roots of the aucurulas, which, like most succulents, spread far in order to catch every drop of moisture. Moreover, it was midday when they began work, the temperature was higher than ever, and the heavy overnight rain had raised the humidity so that they felt that they were breathing pure moisture. For more than an hour, the sweat poured off the three scientists as they worked, crouched over the plants under the near-vertical sun.

When they had at last completed their task, they half collapsed in the shade of the Land Rover's interior, while the newborn midges and mosquitoes and countless other insects of the damp desert flew about them.

Late in the afternoon they roused themselves and, badly bitten but triumphant, they started up the Land Rover, checked their compass course, and headed for the distant encampment of Mata-Mata.

Two days later, they were celebrating the success of their expedition in the same Upington hotel, raising glasses of South African champagne to the aucurula, and promising one another that they must go on safari again.

Dr. Appleby had returned from South Africa glowing with good health and success, and bronzed to the color of the sand of the Kalahari, with one dozen aucurula plants safely stowed in their specially heated container in the passenger compartment of a Boeing Jumbo jet.

Fourteen hours later, he was met at the London airport by representatives from Kew Botanical Gardens who examined his specimens with fascinated interest. They took two of them, and the remainder Dr. Appleby drove north to Manchester. Here, eight were carefully consigned to the succulent arboretum, and the last two—still in their heated case—were driven to Millbeck in the trunk of Dr. Appleby's car.

Before he had left on his expedition to the Kalahari, Dr. Appleby had made sure that his own private arboretum at End House would be ready for use on his return. Jack Williams was an eccentric old recluse, but he had promised that it would be all wired up for heating by the time of his return. But to Dr. Appleby's dismay, it was still not in working order. He was therefore left with the alternative of driving all the way back to Manchester or taking a chance that the precious succulents would be safe until his arboretum was ready.

Fortunately, Cumbria was in the grip of a heat wave, and if this hot weather, which had raised the temperature to a level for his plants to survive out of doors, continued, then he felt safe in planting them temporarily in the orchard.

After a happy, chatty tea with Lucy and Rachel, that is what Dr. Appleby did, close to the wall at the top of the orchard. First he cleared an area of grass with a spade, and then dug two holes, well separated and each of about four times the size of the succulents' pots. Into these holes he worked a generous portion of the spare Kalahari sand he had taken the precaution of bringing back, and delicately lifted the plants in the plastic bags from the pots, disturbing as little as possible the sand that held their wide-spreading roots. With practiced, loving hands, he tucked them in as if they were twin infants being bedded down for the night.

When he had finished this task, he surveyed the tender little yellow plants lovingly, and thought, "What a transformation for you! From the farthest corner of the Kalahari to this little corner of northern England! I wonder how you'll like it here?"

They were to be the subject of much close study, so they had better survive. But he felt optimistic for their future. Succulents are not all that sensitive, the disturbance in their lives had been minimal, and the temperature here in August was well above what they sometimes endured during winter nights in the desert.

His plants were safe.

Toward the end of that school summer holiday, early in September and with a new heat wave back over Cumbria, Lucy decided that she would take a late afternoon ride up over Craig Fell in the hope of catching a glimpse of the pair of golden eagles. She knew approximately where they nested, high up and inaccessible on a sheer rock face, and the National Society for the Protection of Birds had told her, as a member and in confidence, that it was believed they had two surviving chicks out of three eggs that had recently hatched.

She told Rachel where she was going and promised to be back before it became completely dark.

For several days after her discovery of the object in the orchard she had been slightly nervous about riding alone and had sought out the company of John and her other friends. She had temporarily lost trust in herself and was afraid not of what might happen to her but that she might see something supernatural or unaccountable, without witnesses or proof, and suspect that she might be suffering from illusions. Once was enough!

Later, she had taken herself firmly in hand, given herself a sharp lecture, and taken Balliol off for a long ride.

Now she harnessed and saddled up her pony, whom Lucy suspected of affecting resentment at being taken from his field unexpectedly and so late in the day, and rode off up the bridle path that led over the flank of Craig Fell. She had a cheese sandwich in the saddlebag her father had given her for Christmas, and her precious field glasses were slung over her shoulder.

It took Lucy half an hour to reach the highest point of the bridle path. There she gave her old pony a few minutes' rest, which he occupied in tearing off hazelnut leaves and munching them happily, before she opened a gate which led through a field and then onto the open fellside.

Balliol became suddenly lively at the sight of the open grass and bracken fellside and, with only the suggestion of a squeeze to his flanks, broke into a fast canter and then briefly and marvelously into a full gallop, just as if he were five instead of twenty-five years old.

Lucy drew him up before they reached an area which, she knew well, was covered with rocks half concealed by bracken at this time of the year. She laughed out loud and patted her pony's sweating neck. "Quite the dashing youngster today, aren't we?" she said close against his ear.

She got off and led him up a steep and narrow stony track until they reached an old stone sheep pen, very tumbled down and with a rickety old gate, but secure enough for Balliol while she continued farther for a few minutes on foot. Once inside, he seemed quite content to munch at some rather poor-looking grass and bracken that grew there.

"Back soon—be good," said Lucy. She clambered up the path that led around the summit of Craig Fell a thousand feet above. It was not in the least dangerous, but not suitable for dear old ponies. Later, it brought her to a rocky outcrop from which, suitably concealed, she could lie with her glasses and watch for the eagles on the rocky face of Cairngale, hardly more than a quarter mile distant on the far side of a deep and narrow valley.

Up here, by herself, Lucy felt as much a part of the countryside as the black-faced sheep that nosed quietly in and out of the bracken patches, nibbling all day long at the poor grass. Lying among the rocks with the fells towering above her, Lucy could hear the beck deep below talking happily to itself as it bounded down the valley to join the fat river in the flat land leading to the sea. With satisfaction, she heard, too, the twit of the skylarks that always seemed to keep human company on the fells and, several times, the mournful cry of the curlews that nested secretly in the thickets.

Lucy looked closely at the scarred rock face opposite, and found nothing. She lay still for ten minutes, watching the sky lose the brightness of its blue as the sun neared the horizon. This was a favorite hunting time for predators, with the wind falling and mice and shrews and voles and other tasty prey venturing out.

Two big dark birds came into view at the head of the valley, circling slowly. She trained her glasses on them, and they at once became excitingly large —not large enough at this distance for her to see the birds' eyes, but she liked to imagine them peering downward unblinkingly, scouring the fellside for the slightest movement that might betray a small animal. She could tell by the occasional wing beat that kept them gliding and circling that they were not the eagles. These were buzzards, lovely birds to watch but common around these parts.

The light had begun to fade when she saw the eagles with her naked eyes. She at once swung her glasses onto them with excitement. It was her pride and satisfaction that, besides herself, only a few ornithologists knew they nested here, and that only one or two pairs nested in the whole of Cumbria— the whole of England, some said. They were nearer than the buzzards, and immediately distinctive from them by their large heads and the great spread of their wings, which they held almost flat as they quartered the side of the valley in a long glide. One of them uttered a single shriek, and shortly afterward the other found prey—perhaps an evening rabbit or red squirrel—and dropped like a boulder toward the valley floor. Lucy strained to follow it but lost it against the darkness.

"Oh, you wonderful, lovely great things!" Lucy exclaimed, imagining them returning to their nest on a sheltered rock ledge somewhere on that sheer wall and so tantalizingly close, with prey clutched in their talons for the two ravenous, open-mouthed chicks.

The second bird circled, sometimes briefly disappearing against the fellside and reappearing against the now purple sky. Once it shrieked, and then a few seconds later, shrieked again more shrilly, repeatedly, the cry echoing back with mournful urgency from the rock precipice. Lucy watched it in growing excitement, imagining that it might be about to mob an errant buzzard.

But it was no buzzard that came into view through her field glasses. It was a bird she had never seen before, twice, three, four times larger than the golden eagle, with a barrel-shaped black body and fine transparent wings that were beating too fast to count the rate.

The eagle, shrieking with fury, dived repeatedly at the creature as it flew unconcernedly across the valley in a straight line like some bizarre Chinese kite on a string. Lucy bravely kept her glasses on it, memorizing its features as any good ornithologist must do, until it filled the lenses and the eagle gave up its harassment. Then she put down her glasses and watched, wide-eyed and with hammering heart, as it flew low over her head.

First a pair of stubby antennae, then a small head almost concealed between two enormous black-and-blue bulging eyes, what looked like a fluffy yellow bulge on the back of its hairy, barrel body, and six (or was it eight?) long, multijointed hairy legs that were half drawn into the body like a plane with its undercarriage half retracted. But the most sinister feature of all was the short pointed projection sprouting from the middle of the head, between the unbelievable eyes, like a centaur's horn.

"That's not a bird—not a *bird*!" Lucy told herself

44

desperately. Her mind turned to the big flying model aircraft some of John's friends flew on weekends. Did its steady line of flight suggest that it might be some super-elaborate and super-huge model which had gone astray? But the deep humming sound as it passed over her head, those protuberant eyes, those antennae probing the air ahead—and the speed! That was not the work of schoolboys. Perhaps some secret pilotless new aircraft designed to terrify or mystify an enemy? No, impossible.

Lucy watched the flying creature until it was out of sight against the dusk sky, and suddenly remembered Balliol. Poor Balliol! How he loathed anything unnatural. And nothing could have been more frighteningly unnatural than that huge thing humming low over his head.

She got to her feet and ran back down the path, calling his name when she was within earshot. "Balliol, it's all right, I'm coming."

To her relief, the pony had not broken out, as he could so easily have done. But she saw at once by his eyes and sweating flanks that he had had a nasty shock. She walked him out of the pen and quietly along the path down the fellside in the half light. She talked soothingly to him, but the words she softly spoke did not echo the turbulent state of her own mind.

Twice now, she was thinking. Two strange and frightening things. Both suddenly there, and both suddenly gone. And no witnesses—except an angry eagle and a terrified pony! This time I will tell no one. But what does it all mean? Have other people seen them and been too frightened to tell anyone else? Am I suffering from illusions or just going mad? You can go mad as easily at twelve as any other time, I suppose. And, if I *am* going mad, will my madness be filled with great cylinders that twitch, and weird flying creatures?

What had promised to be a nice, interesting evening ride had suddenly become a nightmare.

But there was worse to come before Lucy got home.

When they reached the bridle path, she had a few words with Balliol to inquire whether he felt steady enough to be ridden. She decided he was, drew down the stirrups, and climbed up onto his familiar, friendly back. He was keen to return to his field and took her at a fast trot, occasionally breaking into a canter.

He was cantering when he suddenly shied, and Lucy was nearly thrown over his head.

"What's the matter now? What have you seen, silly? Nothing at all." Lucy looked up into the dark sky, half expecting to hear again that deep-throated drone and see that horrible shape above. The sky was clear. But not the ground. As Balliol stood as if frozen into stone, Lucy glanced about her. And there, under a young rowan, head on a rock outcrop, brown body lying half across the track like a huge sack, lay a horse.

She knew at once what it was. Several of Mrs. Effingham's brood mares had still not been found. And this was one of them, perhaps taking itself home. She dismounted and approached the prone beast, looking down into her vulnerable face.

In the half light she cound just make out her eye, open and staring at her in terror. There was froth oozing from her mouth, and the swollen-with-foal belly was heaving up and down feebly, as if life was soon to be insupportable.

Poor thing! thought Lucy. She must have tripped and broken a leg—and so near to home. And recently, because she certainly had not been there when she had ridden past an hour ago.

She was about to remount Balliol to go for help when something made her turn back to the sick mare. Again she knelt by the beautiful thoroughbred head, looking down into that one frantic eye. She put her hand on the head as if offering the last rites, and as she did so the mare attemped to get up. But she was past that. She could no longer even raise her head. And suddenly she was still, quite still, eye staring, flanks no longer rising and falling.

To be witness to the death of something as big and precious as a horse was the most moving and awful thing that Lucy had ever experienced. For a few moments its enormity was more than she could believe. But it was true. She had to accept the fact. The life had left this beast while her hand tenderly touched her cheek, the heart had ceased to pump blood, the lungs to pump air, that one eye to see. All this complex and beautiful organism was still. Already the process of putrefaction must be starting. Why? Why? Why?

The tears were streaming down Lucy's face as she

reached for Balliol's reins, and she put her face against his cheek so that her tears mixed with his sweat, and realized that this must one day happen to him, too. "Oh, Balliol!"

Lucy was aghast to meet John a half mile from home. She did not want to see anyone, least of all this friend who had half shared and then doubted her last secret. She was embarrassed and did not know what to say.

John did the talking. He had a flashlight but put it away once he had satisfied himself that he had found her. "Rachel sent me for you," he said. "She's in a state because you said you'd be back before it's dark."

"It isn't dark." Lucy spoke tersely, hoping her tears would not sound through her voice.

"Well, she was worried. What have you been doing?"

"Nothing. Just birds."

He sounded dashed. He had come to be sociable, but now remained silent as he walked beside her, Balliol picking his way with practiced steps along the stone-littered track. It was properly dark between the overhanging hedges near the house. Then they came into the light from the outside lamps which Rachel had switched on.

There was a car standing outside the house, but not her father's. It was a dirty mauve Jensen, Mrs. Effingham's. And Mrs. Effingham was standing beside the open driver's door talking to Rachel.

She looked up at the sound of Balliol's hooves and shaded her eyes against the glare of the porch light. "Is that the Thomson boy?" she asked.

No answer was needed as the pony and Lucy and John all came within the cone of light.

Lucy said, "There's one of your mares up on the Craig Fell bridle path. I'm afraid she's dead, though."

"That's three today." Mrs. Effingham turned and spoke explosively, but then she always talked as if she were a machine gun. "And somebody's going to pay for this." She might have lost £10,000 on the stock market instead of three beautiful brood mares.

Still without a word, John had taken his bicycle from beside the house and begun to pedal away. Mrs. Effingham turned and said again, louder and more pointedly, "Yes, somebody's going to pay for this."

Then she left, in her usual scurry of stones, fumes, and racing engine noise as if it were a ritual of departure that she should offend the three senses at once. She had told Rachel that she would be back to talk to Dr. Appleby.

"That woman!" exclaimed Rachel. "I don't like to think of horses suffering, but if they have to, I'm glad they're hers and no one else's. Now, young woman," she said to Lucy in a practical, more homey voice, "I thought you were to be back before nightfall."

Lucy was unsaddling Balliol. "I'm sorry," she said. "I'd have been back sooner except for the poor dead horse. Oh, Rachel!" she said, dropping the saddle and running to her. "She died in my arms

—my arms, just like that." And she sobbed onto her shoulder, smelling the clean coal-tar soap of Rachel's neck and deriving comfort from the familiar strong arms about her.

"There's something troubling you, Lucy," Rachel said.

"It was terrible. She was so big to die."

"Yes, love, I know. But there's something else. There has been for some time."

"No, I'll be all right." She unhooked herself from Rachel's neck. "I'll just put Balliol away with some oats. What's for supper?"

It was quite dark, a still, starlit night, when she led Balliol down the road to the field gate. He was being very sprightly and kept nudging her arm and trying to get his head into the bucket of oats.

She opened the gate and unclipped the leading rein. A smart crack on his haunch sent him into the field, and Lucy put down the bucket and closed the gate. "Don't spill them," she instructed Balliol. "Greed means waste—you ought to know that by now."

She tied the gate to the post, and had walked a dozen yards when she suddenly stopped, listening. Was it just the echo of a recent fear? Or was that really the same deep drone she had heard during those terrifying seconds on Craig Fell—this time distantly and from across the other side of the valley?

It continued for several seconds before it was overwhelmed by the thunder of Balliol's hooves tearing across his field. Only terror could drive her pony from a bucket of oats. So it had not been her imagination.

When the sound of Balliol's hooves had died and he had, no doubt, sought shelter and comfort in his hut at the far end of his field, there was silence again. Not a sound. Not a sound, not even the cry of an owl, could be heard over all Millbeck.

John said, "I've found your thing."

"What do you mean?" Lucy asked.

"You know, that thing you said you saw in your orchard? That day of the storm."

Lucy caught her breath and stopped stroking Scot, considering the implications and feeling a mixed current of fear and relief run through her. So, whether or not she had really seen that giant flying creature, at least the object in the orchard had not been an illusion. John would have a rational explanation. Or, failing him, her father.

"Where?" she asked.

"Down by the beck. I was testing the water flow for my generator. If you'll give me a hand with the dam we could have hydroelectricity in Millbeck next week."

"What does it look like?" Lucy asked anxiously.

"I'll show you if you like. It must be the same thing, but I couldn't make it move. There are two of 'em."

They went across the fields, with Scot bounding ahead. The heat was less and the sky was filled with broken clouds moving fast from west to east over the fells, brushing the tops of the highest of them.

"Old Docherty died last night," said John. "They found him up by the Yewstone, with two of his sheep dead near him. I expect he was seeing to them when he went."

"He was very old," said Lucy. Poor old Docherty, one of the last of the real shepherds. He had lived more of his life on the fells than in the village, some said.

They worked their way down the beck, which was very low in water and very easy to negotiate, rock to rock. They were below End House, which could just be seen through the trees, white against green, when John stopped.

"They're over there. They were half in the water, but I pulled them out."

Like most becks, Millbeck had little shelving beaches of crushed stone here and there, like coarse sand. They were swallowed up when the beck was in flood and always reappeared when the water fell again. On one of them, under a hawthorn, were two of the brown-gray objects, identical to one another, lying close to the water's edge.

Lucy studied them anxiously from some distance. They had been the subject of so many fearful thoughts, and even nightmares, since that hot morning with Balliol, that she was not going to rush at them now. They looked even bigger lying out there in the open than the one lying in the grass of the orchard.

"Come on, they won't bite you." John was

crouching over them and picked one up as he spoke. "Catch? They're quite light."

Lucy shook her head. Scot, barking loudly and in a boisterous mood, was rushing at them as if they were hedgehogs he had to bully into submission. She plucked up her courage and joined John, looking closely at one of them. It was not quite the same. This had a dead, hollow look to it. And, of course, she suddenly realized, it lacked that curious protuberance and little stump at the narrow end. Some of the sinister quality of the object had disappeared with the loss of that "head."

Feeling more courageous, Lucy put the palm of her hand flat over it. There was no sign of any flexing of the scales, no twitching. "It doesn't move," she said, half relieved, half resentful.

"How can it, silly? It's just a husk—empty, look." He held it up. John was right. It was like a frail, hollow section of old tree trunk washed up on the bank.

"Your father'll know what they are," said John. "We'll take one with us."

"No, leave them here," said Lucy emphatically. "Scientists like to see things on site if they can. It sometimes gives them a clue. They'll be all right here. He's home this evening."

It was true, of course. The less interference the better. But, as well, Lucy had a peculiar distaste for these husks lying by the beck and did not want one of them in her house, or near it for that matter.

Lucy returned the short way to End House, up

53

beside the little ghyll that began below the orchard, while John returned with Scot to Gartholme. When he got there he wished he had stayed with Lucy. The black car was in the yard. "Oh no, not *again*!" he exclaimed in anguish.

"Good morning, sir," said the detective, as friendly as ever, man-to-man, hand extended in greeting. "Your mother kindly said I might just have one more quick word with you. Shall we sit outside, or in the car?" He studied the sky. "It'll be coming on to rain soon."

The car's back door was open, and John stepped in without a word. Scot leapt onto his lap, and that was a comfort.

"We're just having to check on all purchases of Mylodol in the last few weeks. I believe you bought some in Rangarth—let me see . . ." The detective thumbed through a notebook full of names and addresses. "Ah, yes, on the last day of last month. August thirty-first."

John found his voice. "My dad sent me."

"Yes, we realize that, but of course you signed for it, it being a poison and all that." The detective laughed tolerantly. "Very Sherlock Holmes today, aren't we? How many syringes did you buy?"

"I don't know."

"Funny—you mean you don't know what you signed for and how many you brought home?"

John began to speak more easily now that he knew they weren't talking about the padlock any more. "Dad has an account there, you see. I'm always getting things seeing as we've no car and the bus being twenty-five pence each way."

54

"Yes, but how many?" persisted the detective with just a trace of impatience in his voice.

"I don't know. He just handed me a sort of canvas bag with a string pull-together and said, 'Here, this'll keep your dad quiet for a while—specially if he takes 'em all at once.' Something like that. Then he laughed, and I laughed too, and I biked back. That's all. Dad'll know."

The detective opened the door of the car that still smelled of old cigarettes and leather. "No, your dad doesn't know. He just used one to put down a sheep, he says, and hung up the bag in the barn for next time."

When they had gone, John went into the kitchen. His mother looked up anxiously from the stove. "What did you tell them?" she asked.

"I told 'em just what happened. Why do they keep going on at me?"

"They say they're asking everyone who's got Mylodol round here."

"But why, Mum?"

"Seems those brood mares Mrs. Effingham never got back all died of an injection. Seems they had the mark in their necks."

Lucy said, "Come and see, Dad."

"Couldn't you bring one to me here? I've had a long day in the lab. And that drive in the rain's really whacked me."

Lucy did not want to say that she had not dared to pick one up. "You always say to leave things on site," she said. "If you're a proper scientific field worker that is." She had not meant to be cunning, but it was the one provoking challenge that could get him away from his pint of recovery beer and deep armchair.

The rain had stopped and the low sun, long since set on End House, still shone on the beck below and on the far side of the valley.

"Lead on, then, " said Dr. Appleby cheerfully, pulling himself up and draining the last of his pint.

They walked together down the path beside the ghyll. It was Friday evening, the start of Lucy's last weekend before school began. But weekends were always special with a two-day-a-week father.

On the way Dr. Appleby said, "We can get the plants into the arboretum this weekend. Jack's left a note to say we can switch on the heating now. It's time they were inside. An early severe frost could do a lot of damage."

"To the aucurulas?" asked Lucy.

"Well, I'm most concerned about them, of course. But there are other plants in the orchard I want to get inside now. Want to give me a hand with them?"

Lucy said she would. It was always nice working with her father. Unlike some fathers she had met, hers talked all the time, and she was always infected by his enthusiasm. Moreover, it was unusually comforting to have him home; for, however firmly she told herself not to be stupid, she was becoming increasingly uncertain of herself. After two bad frights, she felt strung up in nervous expectation of a third.

They made their way across the stepping-stones and followed the path along the far side of the beck until they reached the point where their own ghyll fed into it.

"It's over on the other side," said Lucy. "About there."

Her father followed her nimbly, rock to rock, pausing once to examine some moss. He always did this when they were out. Like the weather, plant life was always there, a constant source of interest for the specialist wherever he happened to be.

The crossing back was more difficult than before because the beck had risen several inches with the rain and many rocks had been covered. Lucy recognized the place under the hawthorn at once, and ran the last few yards. The little shelving beach had been obscured by the water. The beck was already up to the grass bank above it, gurgling along and complacently unaware of the damage it had caused.

"But they were *here*!" exclaimed Lucy, close to tears. "Great big things, lying just here. Truly they were. John saw them, too. He found them," she continued vehemently, "so I've got a witness, really I have."

"All right, lass, I believe you," said Dr. Appleby soothingly. "Don't take on. They'll no doubt be found lower down."

But they won't, Lucy thought bitterly. Those cunning, evil things would escape, just as they had shown a sign of life to her, but not when John was present.

She held her father's hand on the way back, something she had given up doing a year or two ago. The sun had at last set over the whole valley, and the wind had got up with the dusk, rustling the rowan, sycamore, and oak leaves flanking their path and creating a chorus of sound with the roar of the beck below.

Dr. Appleby was telling Lucy about some simple experiment that he was carrying out. "The stamen was as thick as this stick I'm holding, and we . . ." Suddenly Lucy heard the deep droning sound again. It was distant, but quite clear and so distinctive that Lucy was certain that it was the same sound she had heard already twice before.

Her father went on talking, quite oblivious of the sound, and even when he paused momentarily he made no comment on it although Lucy could hear it more clearly than ever. She was suddenly seized with fear and uncertainty. If it was real, if her ears were not deceiving her, why did her father not comment on it? And if it was an illusion—well, that only proved she was suffering from them, and perhaps she *was* going mad.

The sound continued for several more seconds. It came from the southwest, from over Balliol's field somewhere. Then she caught a glimpse of the great black shape in the sky, briefly and distantly only, but unmistakably. In a flash of awful perception, she remembered the last time she had seen it, and how, minutes later, she had found that dying brood mare. Could there, she wondered, be a connection between those two events she had so recently witnessed?

Without a word, Lucy snatched her hand from her father's, clambered over the stone wall flanking the path, and dashed across the field. Startled sheep scattered on both sides, and her father called after her, "Lucy, Lucy—what's the matter?" She took no notice. Without thought for scratches or bruises, she half jumped over and half tore through a hedge onto the road, sprang over the gate into Balliol's field, and raced up the hill toward his hut at the far end.

Her pony was in a pathetic state of fright again, standing inside his hut, shivering and sweating profusely. She held him around his neck, praying that he would not suddenly collapse as the mare must have done soon after the passing of that flying creature.

She was still with Balliol when her father appeared out of the dusk. She was so worried about her pony that she was unprepared for his question and did not answer at once when he asked what was the matter.

"I—I was worried about Balliol," she replied lamely.

"But why—so suddenly?"

"I just remembered how something awful could happen to him," she said, releasing her arm from around Balliol's neck.

"Well, yes, I suppose so," said Dr. Appleby kindly. "That goes for all of us at any time, come to think of it. But luckily, Balliol seems to be in the best of health, as usual."

To prove his point, the pony walked firmly out of his hut, selected a nearby patch of grass, and began grazing as if nothing had disturbed him in all his life.

As the Amazon estuary draws most of Brazil's water and sends it into the sea, so from the mouth of Mrs. Glover there emerged most of Millbeck's gossip. Sometimes it was true. Sometimes it was not.

Mrs. Glover, it was said, had not left her post office for fifteen years, ever since she had hit two hundred pounds on the scales. Nowadays, her only movements were from till to counter to shelves to back parlor, all at a very measured pace.

She handed John the tin of beans and said, "Your mother will have heard, of course."

John knew what this meant, and sighed. He wanted his breakfast, but first he would have to listen to this latest gossip.

"Your mother'll have heard about Mrs. Effingham's man?"

"No, I don't think so," said John dutifully.

"Really! Well, I thought the whole village knew about that." She settled her vast elbows on the counter and announced with mournful excitement, "One of the junior undergrooms found dead this morning. Along with a stallion." She spoke now in the sepulchral voice she reserved only for really great disasters. "Both dead, man and horse, side by side. Just like that."

"How were they killed?" asked John, his own voice thick with anxiety, and then he realized with relief that surely they could hardly pin a real murder on him.

"No one knows yet. Or else they won't say. It's said the groom had a shotgun beside him, so maybe he wounded his murderer first. That Mrs. Effingham's had armed grooms guarding her stud for three nights now. But guns never did anybody any good."

Dr. Appleby was in a rare bad temper. "Jack's the limit," he said to Lucy at breakfast. "The arboretum's heating doesn't work. He's left out some of the wiring, the silly old fool. And he told me it was ready. It's all very well being an amiable eccentric, but it's very annoying not to be reliable."

He got up from the table and helped clear the dishes. "Be a dear, Lucy, and ride up to his place for me. Tell him I've got to have it working this weekend or I'll be putting a lot of precious plants at risk."

Jack the builder was well known in the village, first for being a dear old boy, second for doing good work as an all-around jobbing builder, third for being unpredictable in his appointments, and fourth for never sending his bills. He lived the life of a semi-hermit in a remote cottage on a track beyond the far end of the village.

Lucy considered the prospect of riding Balliol along that lonely track up the fellside on this dark and cloudy morning, and suddenly realized that she did not relish the idea. "What am I coming to?" she asked herself. There was nothing she used to love more than riding Balliol anywhere, most of all high up on the fells by herself. But now she had lost her nerve—just for the time being anyway. And the reason? She hardly liked to confess it even to herself. But she knew, only too well.

Lucy was becoming increasingly aware that she no longer wanted to stray far from her house, not alone, anyway. The uneasy feeling that she was on the verge of some fearful new threat or challenge continued to nag her. The frightening incidents of the past days had not posed any direct physical threat, but she felt that it was only a matter of time before she became directly involved and directly threatened.

The fear of suffering illusions and losing her reason had returned more strongly than ever, and she dared not tell anyone, no longer from fear of being laughed at, but from fear of being judged unbalanced. "That queer girl, you know, she lives at Millbeck—she has visions, wakes up screaming, I hear." That's what they would be saying. The appalling prospect of special "homes," of special treatment, even of straitjackets, had flitted across her consciousness.

She decided not to take Balliol. Instead, she would go by bicycle in the hope that John would keep her company on his. Even so, she got onto her bicycle reluctantly and pedaled up through the village slowly. Everything looked reassuringly familiar and normal for a while. The whitewashed stone cottages stood as firmly as they had for hundreds of years. Mrs. Rusthwaite's honeysuckle around her porch was flowering as profusely as it had since May. The Thomson cows—thirteen, fourteen, fifteen, yes, all right—were grazing placidly.

The first sign that unusual events were occurring in Millbeck was the police car outside Mrs. Glover's post office. That would give her something to gossip about for days! In fact, the rest of the village was now accustomed to the comings and goings of the police since the release of Mrs. Effingham's horses. Not that their inquiries had produced any results, or so Rachel had told Lucy.

As luck would have it (and Lucy felt that she deserved some), John was keen to accompany her on her errand. He had just completed his hydro-electric scheme, which now lacked only a main switch to be installed in the barn, and that would have to wait until Sam Dodgson drove his van into Barrow.

He took off his overalls and snapped his fingers at Scot as an order to follow. "It's murder in the valley now—according to old gossip Gibson," he said.

"Not Mrs. Effingham?" asked Lucy, trying not to sound excited.

"No such luck. All right, old boy, I like a walk too, but I don't try and eat you every time I go out. No, it was one of the young grooms—armed, Mrs.

Gibson said, too. And one of the best stallions. Both dead. Makes you wonder about old Docherty. They're giving him a postmortem, Mrs. Gibson says."

The collie ran ahead of their two bicycles, picking up interesting scents from time to time, taking a passing interest in any livestock he saw through gates, and barking at a crow which had the cheek to be sitting on a wall.

They were soon well clear of the village, and branched off the road onto the track that led to Jack's cottage. They talked about school, due to start in five days' time, and about their friends and teachers. They were high enough up on the fells here to be close to the base of the scurrying gray clouds, and a faint misty drizzle was falling.

The track wound around a bluff, cutting them off from the village but revealing the lonely head of the valley five hundred feet below—poor, undrained land, this, and used only by Sam Dodgson who usually had a few rough fell ponies grazing on it. Jack's cottage was still a mile ahead.

John broke off in mid-sentence, looking urgently around them. "Where's Scot gone? Hey, Scot!" he called. The collie was still only nine months old and not 100 percent safe with livestock. For a farmer's son to allow his dog to worry sheep would be a shaming thing.

John's whistling had no success either. "I'd better go back. Give me three whistles if he turns up, will you?"

Lucy was suddenly aware of how lonely and wild

it was here, although she had ridden or walked along this track countless times. She leaned against her bicycle and wondered what Jack must feel like returning home late on a winter's night to his cold, solitary cottage.

The misty rain fell intermittently, sometimes concealing the base of the valley and reducing visibility to a hundred yards or less. When it cleared, there was still little enough to see—some scattered rowans down the fellside, a clump of Scots pines, a length of half-fallen wall, the inevitable grazing sheep, and the beck, young and narrow here, twisting its way down toward the village and the foot of the valley.

"Scot! Scot!" Lucy called, the sound of her own voice emphasizing the silence that gripped the fellside.

Then, like a comforting echo, she heard John's distant voice calling his dog.

The drizzle, warm and soft, washed against Lucy's face. A swath of mist passed below her and then lifted to reveal the base of the valley again.

John was whistling for his dog. Or was he? Was that John's familiar whistle? Lucy was doubtful. It was too deep, too continuous. Distant now, but coming closer, closer every second. Surely no human could keep up such a long . . .

Then, like a blow against her heart, Lucy suddenly recognized it for what it was. "Not again!" she appealed in a whisper. "Not again, please. . . ."

But the sound continued relentlessly, loud overhead, louder even than the first time she had heard it. She forced herself to look up. There was nothing but cloud, though she thought she felt a passing breath of wind such as great wings might create. But by now she was capable of imagining almost anything.

The sound began to fade so that she could hear her own heart beating, and breaking out of the cloud a half mile away she saw the flying creature again, black and bulbous, with a touch of gold on its back.

It was flying fast, and on the same dead straight course as before, like a plane on automatic pilot and seemingly beyond its own decision making.

But it did, after all, have a primitive mind of its own and control of its direction, for it suddenly changed course and began to lose height as it diminished in size with distance.

Holding her bicycle with tight-clasped hands, and paralyzed with fear, Lucy watched it aim straight for the black ponies grazing innocently and unconcernedly on the bright green grass at the head of the valley. Like a bomber with its cargo of death, the creature picked out one of them and went fast down on it.

At the last second, the horses, suddenly aware of the threat falling upon them, lifted their heads and stampeded in all directions. But one of them was too late to save itself. The flying creature's target was halted in its tracks as the great lanky legs closed about the horse's body. Lucy saw it stumble and collapse on the ground, and be instantly enveloped, as a scuttling mouse is held by a cat.

Then Lucy screamed.

She had never screamed before. Not like this. And she did not know that she was doing it. The scream, repeated again and again, rose into the mist and cloud and was lost across the face of the fells.

John found Scot. He had a sheep's thighbone. The sheep had not been dead for long, and the decaying flesh was too great a temptation for a young dog with an insatiable appetite. John found him lying beside a young ghyll, crunching the bone in utter contentment. He was furious with the collie and beat him. But he did not beat him in anger. John, coming from countless generations of hill-farming stock, beat him sharply and quickly for discipline and then at once treated him normally and affectionately.

"Drop it! Heel, heel, heel! Good dog!"

Scot cringed in shame and slunk up behind his master's left leg.

At that moment, John heard Lucy's distant scream. He hesitated for about half a second while fears and doubts flashed across his mind. Then he began to run. But the mist had fallen thick about him since he had found Scot, and he was uncertain of the direction.

The scream sounded again, as distantly and as urgently as before. It could only be Lucy, and she was in desperate trouble.

John turned to Scot. "Sit, boy, sit." He looked appealingly into the dog's anxious brown eyes. "Find Lucy, Scot. Lucy, Lucy!"

The collie leaped like a greyhound from its trap

and, nose to the ground, at once disappeared.

John heard nothing for one minute, one awful minute when the screams slowly died and he heard instead a faint whimpering sound. Then Scot was back again, triumphant, overeager to show his master his skill, and disappearing into the mist before John could catch up with him.

"Scot, Scot!" The collie at once reappeared, and suddenly John was beside Lucy. She was standing above her fallen bicycle, not looking at him, her hands to her face, staring into the mist. The drizzle poured unheeded down her face.

"What's the matter? What is it?"

Lucy remained silent, and John said again, "What *is* it?" He was almost as frightened as she appeared to be. He was about to shake her shoulders when she turned her scared eyes on him and asked, "Didn't you hear it—that droning?"

John said, "Yes, I heard a jet, high up."

"No, it wasn't a jet. It was low down, right over my head. Then it came out of the clouds." She pointed into the impenetrable mist.

"What do you mean 'it'?" John asked, cross because he was still scared.

"A huge sort of . . . a great hairy thing with legs. It dived down on Sam Dodgson's horses—just down there, you know."

John did not know. Nor did he know what to say. He held Lucy's arm, while Scot danced around them, pleased with himself, awaiting congratulations.

"Oh John, it just fell on them from out of the

clouds. It must have fallen like that on the mare the other day."

"Come on, Lucy, you've been reading too much sci-fi. Or fairy tales, or some rubbish. Let's get on to Jack's. You've got me feeling all funny."

John picked up Lucy's bike and put her hand on the handlebar, then picked up his own. The drizzle had eased, a brightness shone from above into the valley as if the clouds had thinned and the sun was not too far distant.

"There, look!" Lucy suddenly shouted. "Look, John." Her bicycle fell with a clatter onto the track where it had been lying before, and Scot was still for a moment, assuming the stance of a pointer instead of a sheepdog, as if even his young, undeveloped animal instinct had scented from afar that unnatural things were occurring.

John looked down into the valley. Where, seconds before, the clouds and soft drizzle had obscured everything, now suddenly, crystal clear, the walls and rowans and pines sprang into visibility. A thin shaft of sun like a searchlight bored down from the heavens and picked out the tumbling water of Millbeck and the whole valley as far as the eye could see was open to his eyes.

Dodgson's ponies were there all right, all but one of them crowded into a corner of the small field. John had difficulty in counting them, but he thought there were six standing under the old yew tree near the Yewstone where they had found Docherty dead the other day.

There was one more in the middle of the splash

of green. John could not at first identify it as a horse because, crouched over it and almost obscuring it, was a huge, bulbous object, sprawled out with wings folded and head seemingly dipped forward like a Concorde's snout and half buried in the unfortunate horse's neck.

PART TWO

"Now do you believe me?" Lucy demanded softly, almost out of breath from holding it.

"Of course I do. And we must tell everyone, quickly. That thing, whatever it is, has got to be killed." John continued to stare in the direction of the scene of carnage, although once again the mist and drizzle obscured the valley floor and everything else more than fifty yards from them.

They mounted their bicycles and began pedaling, side by side, fast down the track toward the village, Scot bounding behind them. Lucy's mind was in a state of confused terror and anger. She thought back to the brood mare whose head she had held as she died, and of the other horses who had died so horribly, of harmless old Docherty and the young groom and the sheep. Where would this murderous flying creature strike next? Its taste obviously ran to horseflesh, and that meant . . .

"John, now we know, we *must* tell Mrs. Effingham," Lucy said.

For a moment John was tempted to say, "No, the

more horses she loses the better." But his better nature took over, and instead he said, "OK—I'll help Dad in with the herd. Everybody'll have to get their stock under cover. It's the only chance."

But the sequence of events was not as simple as that. A year earlier, when Lucy had been taken on a rare visit to her father's laboratory in Manchester, they had called on one of Dr. Appleby's friends at the university, an entomologist called Austin Barber—or "A.B." A.B. was a bit of a wag. On his desk was a sign which had amused Lucy. "The possible I'll do today," it said. "The impossible may take a little longer."

Dr. Barber had seen Lucy's interest and had explained jocularly: "When someone brings me in a dead bug with twelve heads and says, 'What's that, Doc?' I just turn that sign toward him."

Lucy was to learn, in the course of the next hour, that A.B.'s sign could apply to that flying killer, or at least to people's belief in its existence. It was going to take longer than that to make people believe in the impossible.

Lucy freewheeled onto the wide sweep of gravel in front of Mrs. Effingham's house. She had never ventured in here before, nor seen at close hand the hideous mock Elizabethan house with its bright blue front door and window frames. She caught a glimpse through the windows of elaborate chandeliers and fumed oak paneling. Then, even before she could dismount, a man's voice called out crisply, "What is it, young lady?"

Lucy stopped and got off. A middle-aged man in jodhpurs was striding across the gravel. Lucy recognized him as Mrs. Effingham's head groom, a man of great power and responsibility on the stud farm but, according to John, as unpleasant a piece of work as his mistress.

"I wanted to see Mrs. Effingham, please," said Lucy.

"She's not back yet. What did you want to say to her?" The groom eyed her with suspicion and disfavor, as if only Mrs. Effingham counted as a human and all others were inferior to horses. He had protruding light blue eyes and a fine, carefully trimmed moustache.

"John Thomson and I have just seen one of Dodgson's ponies being killed. I came to warn Mrs. Effingham to get her horses under cover."

The groom looked her up and down as if she might have been a knock-kneed nag fit only for the knacker's yard. "And why under cover, young lady?"

"Because it was killed by a great flying creature, with a huge great body like a barrel, and hairy, too. Like nothing I've seen before—though actually I have seen it twice—just before it killed one of your brood mares."

The more the expression of disbelief on the groom's face grew, the faster Lucy felt impelled to talk, until she found herself quite unnecessarily describing the creature in detail. ". . . and it's got six legs and two huge antennae, and a hooked proboscis for jabbing into . . . and, and, it just fell on the poor pony, it was awful."

The groom interrupted her flow in the powerful and severe voice he used to reprimand his staff from a distance. "Young lady, I'm not used to having my leg pulled by *anyone*, least of all by a lying schoolgirl. You don't seem to realize that this is a serious and tragic matter." His eyes bored into her. "Now you get off back home—your father'll hear about this."

"But it's true—it's true, I tell you." Lucy bicycled away, still protesting, but now with tears of righteous indignation pouring down her cheeks. Halfway around a blind corner she nearly collided with a car. It was going very fast, and she caught a glimpse of mauve bodywork. When she looked over her shoulder she recognized Mrs. Effingham's Jensen, its top down as always when it was not raining. If only beautiful horses were not the victims, how she would like to see misfortune strike that woman again and again until she finally left the valley once and for all!

In order to reach End House, Lucy had to pass Gartholme Farm. John was waiting for her at the entrance, a woebegone figure. "They didn't believe me," were his first words when Lucy drew up beside him. "My own father and mother, they didn't believe me," he repeated, as if he did not believe their own disbelief.

"What did they say?"

"Oh, they weren't nasty or cross. And they didn't think I was deliberately lying. But my dad said the light plays strange tricks on the fells, especially in weather like this. And he told me how he had mistaken a sheep for a giant boar one winter's evening when he'd been a boy and his father had sent him after a hurt sheep."

"But we *both* saw it," protested Lucy.

"I know. But my mum said something about the power of suggestion."

"Well, I like that," retorted Lucy indignantly. Mrs. Thomson, her own beloved Mrs. Thomson, talking as if she'd given John chicken pox or something. "Get your bike. My father'll understand. Especially if you're there too."

Lucy took the precaution of putting Balliol into his shed and closing the lower half of the door on him before they went into End House. Dr. Appleby was in his new arboretum, his back to the door, examining some soil in a pot. He did not look around when Lucy came up behind him, but he heard her and said, "I got tired of waiting, so I've done the job myself. It's working now."

"We never got to Jack's place," said Lucy. "You see, we . . ."

"That's good, then. What kept you?"

Lucy was suddenly overwhelmed and silenced by the importance of this moment. Surely, she told herself, her beloved, trusting, trusted father would believe her.

"Well?" Dr. Appleby put down the pot he had been holding and turned around to the pair of them. "Well, what's the matter—you're both looking very guilty," and he laughed.

"We saw a pony being killed," Lucy began. She looked at John who said under his breath, "Go on, you tell."

"It was near Jack's place, and I heard a noise. It was the same droning noise I heard when I ran away from you last night. I'd heard it before that, too. And I'd seen what—what made it. It was being mobbed by the golden eagles, but it was much bigger than them—much, much bigger. Like a great barrel but flying terribly fast, and droning as it went.

"John didn't see it at first. Then the clouds cleared and we both saw it. It was terrible." Lucy hesitated, then forced herself to go on and to be clear and concise so that her father would understand and believe her. And she did well. She did not dare to look at her father's face, but she had a feeling he was taking it all in. When she stopped talking, John intervened and added to her description. He sounded serious and responsible.

"I see," said Dr. Appleby. "Must have given you a bit of a turn." Lucy looked at him now, and she might have thrown herself into his arms if John had not been there. He was smiling. But there was no trace of doubt in that smile, and the eyes that glanced from one to the other of them expressed complete belief.

Dr. Appleby reached for the telephone and dialed a ten-digit number. "Is that you, A.B.? Sorry to dig you out of your bug-ridden home on the weekend, but you're wanted up here at Millbeck. I think we have a case of some sort of gigantism on our hands. Yes, deadly. . . No, not just animals. Humans, too. *Homo sapiens,* yes. Put your foot down hard on that old jalopy, will you?"

He put down the telephone and turned his attention back to Lucy and John. "Very rum business," he remarked musingly, scratching his head. "Very rum indeed. Tell me again about those things you found down by the beck, the ones that mysteriously disappeared as soon as I got near them."

"They were the same, but not quite the same, as the thing I found in the orchard," said Lucy.

"I don't know about that. Why didn't you tell me? Did you know?" he asked, turning to John.

"Yes, but it had disappeared as soon as I got near it."

"But you did see the things in the beck, so it's not just Lucy's description we're relying on?"

John confirmed that he had, and described them roughly as he remembered them. Then Dr. Appleby said, "Strange—very strange, how they seemed to move about."

Then Lucy suddenly remembered the storm that had followed her discovery in the orchard, and the heavy rain that had caused the beck to rise and sweep away the evidence. She told her father, adding, "So they might not have moved about themselves. They could have been swept away *both* times. And yet the first one I saw wasn't quite the same as the second two."

"How's that?" asked her father.

She explained how the object in the orchard had

twitched under the proximity of her hand, and that it had a horrible sort of extension, almost like a head, while the one she had examined with John was hollow and lifeless, just a skin.

Dr. Appleby pondered this information and then picked up the telephone again, dialing only three numbers this time, 9-9-9. "I think the time has come to talk to the police. In fact, there isn't any time to waste."

Lucy and John heard the crisp voice at the other end ask, "Police, ambulance, or fire?"

"Police," said Dr. Appleby, and in a second he was through and talking seriously, swiftly, and precisely to an officer. Even the sharp rap at the door did not break the flow of his account. Lucy answered it instead, and was appalled to see the square-set figure of Mrs. Effingham on the porch. She did not have the opportunity of greeting her, or of saying anything, and the tentative smile she had assumed, as one does for anyone at the door before opening it, was wiped from her face by the venom of Mrs. Effingham's words.

"Young woman," she began, her face a mask of fury, "my groom has told me of your practical joking. If you consider the death of thoroughbred horses a subject for joking, then you must have a very twisted mind. Moreover, I am increasingly of the opinion that it is also a criminal mind and that you are in conspiracy with that odious Thomson boy who the police are convinced has been killing my brood mares, and now a prize stallion, with Mylodol injections."

The woman scarcely paused for breath, and moved implacably forward all the time, so that Lucy was forced to retreat into the hall and Mrs. Effingham (for the first and last time) crossed the threshold of End House. "Ah, there is that young criminal and murderer, too, now," she continued when she spotted John, who was standing with an expression of astonishment on his face at the door of the living room. "I hope you realize that you have disgraced your father, and bankrupted him, too, and that you will certainly be spending the rest of your boyhood in a special school for criminals. Unfortunately, they can't order a good whipping as they used to do. So I will take it upon myself . . ."

Mrs. Effingham, beside herself with rage, reached a hand toward the umbrella stand in which several walking sticks rested, and grasped hold of one, at the same time advancing threateningly upon John.

"Daddy!" Lucy shouted suddenly. But Dr. Appleby was already in the hall beside John, staring in amazement at the scene of Mrs. Effingham with his walking stick raised above John's head.

"Put that down!" he ordered, and at the same time laid a protecting arm above John's head. "What do you imagine you are up to? I haven't even invited you into my house."

Mrs. Effingham paused in front of the boy and the man, and Lucy could see that she was actually shaking with fury. "And I did not know that I had invited your daughter onto my land."

"I don't know what you're talking about," said

Dr. Appleby, "and I would be obliged if you would explain this extraordinary behavior."

Mrs. Effingham had lowered the stick and stuck it back into the stand like a frustrated warrior returning a sword to the scabbard. "I don't suppose you do. You're away most of the time, failing to apply any discipline in your home."

Dr. Appleby began to protest, but Mrs. Effingham continued, disregarding him. "I am sure you are not aware that this boy here, as badly brought up as your daughter, purchased a number of syringes of Mylodol after breaking open the gate into my brood mares' paddock and letting them loose. I don't suppose you know, either, that he has used these syringes to destroy some of my best horses, including a prize stallion last night. Nor do you know Dr. Appleby, that your daughter, in order to cover up the crimes of her friend, has been spreading fantastic tales of some giant flying creature, imagining that intelligent adults will believe this creation of her twisted imagination has been responsible for the deaths in this valley—and of humans, too, not just animals."

At this point, Dr. Appleby stepped toward the woman, holding up a hand in protest. "Mrs. Effingham, I must really ask you . . ."

But again, he was outvoiced. Mrs. Effingham continued her diatribe as if he had never opened his mouth. "And now the final straw, the reason why I am here—you will certainly not have heard of this. Let me tell you," she went on, as if anyone could possibly stem the flow, "this child of yours, after describing this fabulous flying bug, or whatever she calls it, to my head groom, then tries to lend credence to it by first saying that she saw it kill a pony, and then—if you please—planted on my land a papier-mâché replica of it."

Even this hard, ruthless, insensitive woman could not fail to notice the sudden breath of silent astonishment with which this news was met by all three of her audience. Then Dr. Appleby said, "I don't think any of us quite understands what you are saying. Are you feeling quite well, madam?" His voice was like spring water on the fells in midwinter.

"Oh, yes," went on Mrs. Effingham, seemingly unaffected by the intervention. "We all know what Miss clever-puss can do with her hands, from the fete. Well, she has excelled herself this time. You just come and see for yourself, lying in my upper field and scaring off my staff, to say nothing of my horses. Only hurry, Dr. Appleby, because the police'll be here shortly to take away these young criminals. And that's only the start of it. It's perdition for you, young lady."

Mrs. Effingham turned and made straight for the door, without even glancing at Lucy as she marched past. Dr. Appleby followed hard behind her. He was saying, with equal defiance, "The police have better things to do at present, Mrs. Effingham. I have just been speaking to them, and they tell me that . . ."

Dr. Appleby was cut short by the slamming in his face of his own front door. In a few seconds they heard the engine of Mrs. Effingham's Jensen being started, the offbeat of its V8 engine as she revved it up and then tore away down the road.

He turned to Lucy and John. He was very pale but was smiling encouragingly at them. "Well, everything is happening this weekend and no mistake. Cheer up, you two. I think she must have gone mad." He walked back into the living room, Lucy and John at his heels.

"What were you going to say when you were so rudely interrupted?" asked Lucy.

Dr. Appleby was pouring himself a substantial whiskey. "I was going to say that the health authorities have completed their postmortems on old Docherty and the young groom who was killed last night. It always takes a bit of time, but the results are through. Also the vets report on two of the horses."

"What do they say?"

"They all say the same thing. Death was caused by the sudden nonfunctioning of the heart."

"Why?" asked Lucy. "They must know why the heart suddenly stopped."

"Due to lack of blood," said Dr. Appleby. "As simple as that."

The giant corpse lay close to a stone wall in one of Mrs. Effingham's upper fields. You could only explain away any object as impossible as this by telling yourself that it must be man-made, that it must be a practical joke. Lucy and John admitted to one another that they could not have believed it to be a real corpse if they had not seen it in its living form.

It lay flattened on the grass fifty yards away, its six multijointed hairy legs spread out at all angles like collapsed scaffolding, its tubby dark body, which Lucy judged to be about the size of a small car, sagging over to one side like a Christmas balloon past its best, the dark hairs as lifeless as those of a sickly dog.

One of the diaphanous wings was half crushed, the other lay limp and half drawn in to the body. The head, which was attached by what looked to be the flimsiest of threads, had conformed to the general tilt of the corpse, and only one great eye, all its color gone in death, stared sightlessly up to the sky from which the monster had made its final descent.

Dr. Appleby tried to approach closer but was halted politely by a policeman, who had also held back several curious villagers. "It's amazing to think of it actually flying," Dr. Appleby said to Lucy. "No wonder you were scared. But somehow it has lost its venom, lying there like unwanted rubbish."

After her past frights, Lucy did not care for the sight of the dead insect. But she forced herself to look at it again, as a good scientist should, casting her eyes over it, and even resorting to her field glasses to examine it with more care.

She was not satisfied with what she saw. It was a corpse all right, not a papier-mâché replica as Mrs. Effingham had grotesquely claimed. But there was something wrong with it, all the same, even if she was unable to define it.

Her father said, "It's like something out of a Grimm's fairy tale. We'd better get back to A.B. He's going to have the time of his life up here."

Lucy put away her glasses with relief, but still not satisfied, and joined John and her father in the walk to the car.

It was a comfort to be back at End House, and to see the familiar, friendly head of Balliol in the distance peering out from his hut at the end of his field. She must take him up some hay and oats, she reminded herself.

Dr. Barber had already arrived, having evidently responded to Dr. Appleby's appeal to put his foot down. The old, battered car, a 1952 Hillman Minx, must have made good time up the motorway from Manchester. He had let himself in, and was studying Dr. Appleby's arboretum, twinkle-eyed and smiling just as Lucy remembered him.

But when he listened to the account of the appearance and activities of the giant flying creature, his face assumed the serious expression of a doctor recording symptoms before delivering a diagnosis.

"It's obviously very important to know, from the practical and scientific points of view, if the dead giant insect is the same as the one you, Lucy, have twice or three times seen flying. You tell me that once it came low, close over your head. As an ornithologist, you would have noted all its characteristics carefully. Now, if they are one and the same, then it is likely that there is only one specimen and that our troubles are over. But. . ."

As Dr. Barber continued, Lucy frantically searched her mind for a clear picture of the creature as it had flown above her up on Craig Fell. She even remembered saying to herself, I must remember every detail—it is important not to miss anything. . . . But it was so difficult to compare in her memory the configuration of it above her on that terrifying evening, and again, crushed and lifeless lying in that field an hour ago.

What was it her father had said? "Somehow it has lost its venom." Venom. Yes, of course, that was it. Triumphantly, rushing her words, Lucy exclaimed, "I know. I remember now. It didn't have a proboscis. It had lost it. That's it," she ended, smiling all over her face.

"You're sure?" asked A.B.

John broke in to say, "I didn't see it in the air. But this morning, when it was killing that pony, it seemed to be digging something into its neck."

"That's bad," said the entomologist firmly.

"Why bad, A.B.? It might have crushed it as it died, like a plane smashing in its nose." said Dr. Appleby.

A.B. shook his head. "I'm afraid not. What we seem to have here is a species of bloodsucking insect that has experienced some freak metamorphosis during the egg or larval stage.

"A large number of species of mosquito and midge mate right after emerging from the pupal stage. The female has to have blood before she can lay. Then the male dies, almost immediately. He has no means of remaining alive because he lacks the female's proboscis.

"I fear, then, that the insect that lies dead across the valley had recently mated, and that if a number of eggs have not already been hatched, they soon will be.

"So, even if we succeed in destroying those at present alive, there may well be hundreds more still to come. Unless, of course, we can destroy them as eggs or larvae or pupae."

Nobody spoke for some seconds. Lucy turned her eyes first to her father. He was sitting beside Dr. Barber, who had himself drawn a notebook from a pocket and was writing in it, making with his pen the only sound to be heard in the room.

Lucy felt in her bones that this was a moment of truth she would remember all her life—the moment when the fate of the valley was decided.

Why, she asked herself, had lovely Millbeck—a valley which had known so little violence, so little conflict even, until the malign Mrs. Effingham had set up her stud farm ten years ago—why had Millbeck been chosen as the victim of this fatal frolic of nature? Why here? Why nowhere else?

The near silence was broken by her father's voice asking, "Is there no good news you can give us, A.B.?" And the entomologist gave a bitter laugh.

"Not really. We're dealing here with a giant bloodsucking midge or mosquito which has come from goodness knows where and will be breeding fast, especially in damp, hot weather. How we destroy it I can't begin to think. The only good news if you can call it that, and it doesn't help us here, is that most species of these insects never stray far from their breeding ground. That's probably why there has been no report of them from anywhere else in Cumbria."

A.B. rose from his chair and put away his notebook. "Let's go and look at this corpse. And I suppose this is one occasion when I won't need my microscope."

Outside End House the sky was darker and the clouds lower than ever. A day that had begun with intermittent drizzle was turning dour and thundery, in keeping with the events. They piled into A.B.'s old Hillman, which started with a series of pistol-like cracks and lurched in reverse into the middle of the road. Here the engine died and refused to recover what little life it possessed. Muttering crossly, he got out, brandishing a crank which he inserted under the radiator and wound rapidly. But still there was no response.

At this point, a police car came up the road, blue light on its roof flashing urgently. Dr. Appleby told Lucy and John to get out. "We'll have to do some pushing," he said. "We can't hold up the law."

The police had piled out of their car, too. There were four of them, one of them the detective who had interrogated John. They were not pleased at being held up. An inspector spoke for them all. "This is no time to block the road," he said.

87

"It's not my choice—not the time or the place," replied A.B. breathlessly, applying himself to the crank again.

"I'm sorry about this," said Dr. Appleby. "We're on our way to see the giant insect corpse. You see . . ."

"No one's going anywhere in this village just now, sir. I'm sorry," said the inspector firmly.

"We're both scientists, officer. Dr. Barber here is one of the world's leading entomologists. It's absolutely essential . . ."

"All right, sir," interrupted the inspector again. "We'll take you over there ourselves. But for the present everyone's staying indoors for their own safety."

"Has there been more trouble?" asked Dr. Appleby anxiously.

"Well, we don't want any panic, sir, you understand. But seeing as you and the professor here may be able to help, perhaps you should know. Two more people out in the fields have been attacked and killed this morning. A gentleman walking on the fells has been found dead. And there are a lot of dead sheep about. So any countermeasures your professor friend here can devise are needed urgently."

The inspector turned to Lucy and John who had been helping to get the old car off the road. "Inside with you two. You'll be all right in your own house, but don't leave it."

The detective gave John a wink and a smile. "You're in the clear now, lad. We've traced that

88

spot of bother with the gate to a lad in Carlisle. He was a groom with Mrs. Effingham. She sacked him for impertinence. Besides," he continued briskly, raising his eyes to the sky, "we have, as the saying goes, bigger fish to fry—or rather bugs to kill."

Dr. Appleby was the last to get into the police car. "You do as the inspector says, Lucy. We'll be back soon. Busy yourself making some lunch. I'll get word to Mr. Thomson that John's here."

The police car accelerated away, and as the first clap of thunder sounded over Millbeck, John and Lucy closed the front door of End House behind them. They did not yet know it but, by chance, freak, stormy weather in the Kalahari had set in motion events that were now to be influenced by an equally ferocious and exceptional storm here in west Cumbria.

Many years had passed since Millbeck had last been a beleaguered village. It was around 1640 that the Moss-troopers had made their last assault, coming over the border from Scotland, intent on pillage and cattle, and women if they could get them. It was then that John Thomson's ancestors had driven their livestock into the shippons under their stone houses, barred their doors, and manned their narrow windows with muskets and bows. Then no one would venture outside until the raiders had made off.

Now another Thomson was confined indoors by other raiders. But John had no intention of remaining here at End House. Like a good Cumbrian of any century, he was concerned for his family's livestock.

"I've got to go and see about the cows, Lucy," he said urgently, almost as soon as the door was shut. "And Scot may be out, too. If only Mum and Dad had believed me, they could all be in the barn now."

"You mustn't go," said Lucy. "This is serious, John. That policeman wasn't making it up. Three people dead today, and that groom. It's stupid to go outside."

"It'll kill my dad if his cows are killed. It'll bankrupt him, too."

Lucy said sharply, "And it'll kill your mum and your dad if *you* get killed."

"You can hear them coming," said John. "You said so yourself, and then you can run for shelter."

As confirmation of the dangers outside, they both clearly heard the deep droning sound of an approaching giant insect. It seemed to come right over End House before the sound began to fade and, almost at once, to be replaced by a fresh drone, even louder than the first.

Lucy and John ran to the window. Higher up than they had expected, and flying just below the base of the dark clouds, two well-separated insects flew from north to south across the valley, huge, black, and sinister. In both cases, short spidery antennae probed the air ahead, and Lucy even caught a glimpse of the sharp pointed proboscis of the second.

"Now you see why you mustn't go," said Lucy. "It's suicide."

"Not at all. It makes it all the more necessary for me to try to save our cows," said John tersely. He made for the hall, and before Lucy had a chance to say more, he slammed the front door behind him.

No Millbeck villager could fail to sense the new, doom-laden atmosphere that hung over the fields and houses. No one was to be seen along the road, nor working in the gardens or the fields. Most of the stock had been brought in, too, and some of the villagers had even locked up their hens. In their place, police, reinforced by soldiers, were posted at intervals along the road, some in cars, others wearing tin hats out in the open, all of them armed with rifles. Outside Mrs. Glover's post office, a fully manned army personnel carrier was parked, no doubt signifying to Mrs. Glover the importance the army rightly judged was her due.

Millbeck appeared as if it was expecting a mass invasion by some enemy—a descent of paratroopers instead of some bloodsucking midges or mosquitoes that had suffered a freak metamorphosis.

John pedaled as fast as he could go, ignoring the shouts to stop and get under cover, and dodging the attempts by several uniformed figures to halt him forcibly. The entire herd was in the field. John counted them as he raced past—fourteen, fifteen. All were lying down awaiting the rain that was heralded by another fierce clap of thunder as John turned into the yard.

Scot was there, cowering in the corner under the barn. He hated thunder. But John was firm with him. He needed all the help he could get to move the herd to safety. "Come, Scot!" he called out. "Good boy, come."

He threw down his bicycle and opened the gate to the field. He did not want his parents' help. They would be too slow if there was an attack. He must do this on his own—and quickly. Something had stirred up the insects—perhaps it was the storm, or simply that many more had hatched. But there was no time to spare. Between the rolling thunder blasts, he could hear that deep sinister droning, sometimes far away, sometimes near, sometimes fading, sometimes increasing in volume—but always there, and always the overture to death for some warm-blooded creature in the valley.

A voice from the road above was calling out, "Get under cover—get under cover, you." John looked toward it, but saw that it was not directed at him—it was calling Lucy, who was running diagonally across the field from the far end toward the nearest cows under a big oak tree.

What was she doing here, the stupid girl? John added his own voice to the policeman's. "Get indoors, Lucy!"

She took no notice at all. She was already hitting one of the cows with a stick to get her to her feet. As soon as she had succeeded she turned to another. She was shouting at them and waving her arms—"Go on, on, on. Go on, on, on!" just as Mr.

Thomson would cry to get them into the milking barn.

John and Scot raced up beside her, John still calling to her to get inside. All he got in reply was, "Go and get Madge over there—she's being left behind!"

Scot had not been trained for cattle, but he seemed to sense the gravity of the situation and bravely overcame his fear of the thunderclaps to hustle the cows to their feet and across the field toward the barn.

Once John heard the deep drone of an insect very close above, and he thought he heard a rifle shot through the thunder; but the droning faded, and he gave his mind and energies to getting the cows through the gate. From there they went steadily on their own, by long habit, straight into the barn.

The first rain was falling in heavy drops, and lightning splashed over the valley as if one of the insects was taking a flash photo before attacking. John got what he thought was the last of the cows through the gate, smacking her rump with a stick, and with Scot yapping at her heels.

But where was Lucy? He thought she was already out of the field. He looked back, and to his horror saw that she was still a hundred yards away, struggling with the reluctant Madge.

Then the sequence of events accelerated until they were occurring so rapidly that it was difficult to piece them all together correctly after they were over. First he saw two policemen and a soldier with a rifle leaping over the stone wall from the road, and then running toward Lucy, at the same time that John himself, with Scot in front of him, began his run toward her.

In that split second it was the joint intention of all three men, and of John, to carry off Lucy forcibly and get her under cover. But a moment later the situation had changed and become much more desperate. The arrival of the insects must have been drowned out by a long clap of thunder, because the first that anyone knew of the attack was the sudden rapid descent from the dark clouds above of an even darker shape, legs splayed out, wings vibrating at a great rate, and—most sinister of all—eyes swiveled down and aiming with the sharp-pointed proboscis straight at the cow and the girl.

Then John could hear the deep droning of the insect, like the hum of his biggest electric motor, as it dropped the last few feet onto the cow. Punctuating it was the sound of shots—one, two, three cracks, another deeper explosion, then two more; and as he ran he saw the two policemen firing with handguns, and the soldier behind them firing rapidly with his rifle.

He saw, too, that the shots were striking home. As the insect settled on the cow, the hairy legs gripping its flanks and bearing it down to the ground, the bullets ripped through the wings and into the body, scattering bits like gale-torn clothes from a wash line.

John could not see Lucy. The dark bulk of the insect obscured her. But as he covered the last yards, he caught a glimpse of her again. She had not fled. To John's horror, she was belaboring the insect, beating its side in an effort to make it slacken its grip before the deadly proboscis jabbed into the cow's neck.

She succeeded, too. The shooting had ceased anyway as soon as the men saw how dangerously close she was. But to John, it was Lucy's determined flailing of her stick rather than the firing which forced the insect to raise its body from the prostrate cow. It stood on its six legs over its intended victim for a second, and then rose in the air, damaged wings vibrating too fast for the eye to follow, like a vertical-takeoff fighter plane.

In a moment it was below the cloud base, droning fast across the valley in search of less viciously defended prey.

The two policemen were holding Lucy's arms as if she were some Victorian grande dame about to swoon. "Of course I'm all right," she answered their inquiries. "But let's see how poor Madge is."

The cow looked in bad shape. She was lying in the grass, head still, eyes rolling with fear. Worst of all, there was blood on her side—thick, deep-red blood that was spilling down slowly to the udders. Then, with a stab of mixed horror and relief, Lucy realized that it was not Madge's blood but the blood of the insect's earlier victim, which had spilled out from one of the bullet wounds—the blood of another cow perhaps, or a sheep, or a horse, or even a human being. Who could tell?

The shooting, the shouting, the droning of the insect, had alerted others in the village. More than a dozen armed police and soldiers had arrived at the field, and others were climbing the wall from the road, all with their guns at the ready. At the windows of two of the houses overlooking the field, villagers were looking out anxiously.

The noise had brought out Mr. and Mrs. Thomson, too. Ignoring instructions to keep inside, the couple were running toward the group in the center of the field, calling out, "John, Lucy, are you all right?"

They found no casualties, no evidence of damage except to the assailant itself. For, when no one was looking, the cow had got to her feet, walked slowly away to a quieter spot with better grazing, and when Lucy next saw her, was tearing at the grass in complete contentment. The only sign of her ordeal was the red patch across her flank and the steady dripping of blood onto the ground near her rear hooves.

The brief struggle at Gartholme Farm was over. But it was not the only extraordinary and dramatic event in Millbeck that Saturday afternoon in September as the thunder of a great storm echoed between the fells. Lightning brought blinding flashes of light where near darkness prevailed, and roaming giant insects brought death with their insatiable appetite for blood.

Up on the fells above Jack the builder's lonely

cottage, George Matthews tried to bring his sheep down to a pen near the road, where he planned to stand guard over them with a shotgun. His wife had begged him to stay with her, but he had gone off with his dog, an expression of mixed obstinacy and determination on his lined, brown face.

When he returned three hours later, he was six sheep short, and a changed man—and the rest of his flock were still on the fells, vulnerable to renewed attacks. George Matthews was a firm believer in logic who went to church on Sunday but believed the Old Testament was a tissue of fairy tales.

But like others, he had seen the impossible, and he had experienced fear he had never known before, even in Normandy in 1944 when he was still a young man and a corporal in the Lancashire Yeomanry. On the next Sunday, and for many Sundays after, he took his wife to early morning Mass as well as the eleven o'clock service, and started to read the Old Testament again.

A smart-aleck tourist and his wife, who were staying at Coniston and had planned to explore the Millbeck valley that day, arrived at Rangarth at noon and followed the signposts pointing to the village. But five miles from Millbeck they were halted by soldiers who had thrown a barrier across the road. Along with a dozen other motorists, they were told that army exercises prohibited them from going farther.

But this tourist was determined to outsmart the

army, who had no business to close public roads like this. Being a well-organized fellow, he had brought with him a I:25,000 ordnance survey map, which he used to his temporary advantage by discovering a bridle path which allowed him to join a tarred lane leading up the valley on the opposite side to the main road.

He parked his car in a disused quarry, and after putting on raincoats, the couple began to walk toward the village from the southwest, pleased with themselves that they had outwitted interfering authority.

A mile farther on, they were forced to shelter under some larches from a heavy downpour. In ordinary circumstances, the husband would have suggested returning to the car as the weather was so unpromising. But after that earlier brush with authority, this tourist was determined to reach his original destination, come hell or high water.

Exactly twelve minutes later, as they emerged from a spinney and were descending toward the stepping-stones that span the Millbeck below End House, the wife looked up after hearing an unfamiliar sound above. She was walking some ten yards behind her husband, as usual, and when she called out he did not hear her at first. When he did turn around it was too late. From a pleasant if rather wet walk up a lovely Cumbrian valley, the tourist who was not to be foiled by a bunch of soldiers found himself thrust into a real-life nightmare in which his wife was tumbled to the ground as if struck by an avalanche, and with terrifying speed and decisiveness, a dark monster from the sky had thrust something sharp into her neck, killing her instantly and soundlessly.

A little more than a mile away, desperate events were occurring on Mrs. Effingham's land, and to Mrs. Effingham. It was beyond the ability of either Mrs. Effingham or her head groom to accept even to themselves that they had been wrong. It was nevertheless an indisputable fact that they had been warned of imminent danger by a twelve-year-old girl, and not only disregarded it but falsely accused her of making trouble. The discovery of the male insect corpse could have been a further warning. But arrogance and bitterness are a dangerous combination, and it was not until the officer commanding the two platoons of infantry ordered to Millbeck had personally called at the house that Mrs. Effingham gave instructions to bring all her horses into the stables.

It takes longer to bring in horses than cows or sheep, especially high-strung thoroughbreds. They require coaxing and tempting by people the horses know, while sheep are easily frightened and anxious to please anyway. By the time the storm broke over Millbeck, and the giant insects had begun to roam in search of prey in numbers, as if thunder provided the right accompaniment to their assaults, two stallions and half a dozen mares were still loose in the open fields. Mrs. Effingham and her head groom were both barking orders to junior grooms who were attempting to get near enough to the horses to seize their halters.

This drama could be seen from Gartholme Farm, where Madge was now safely in her stall with the rest of the herd. Mr. and Mrs. Thomson were back in their house, Mrs. Thomson brewing up some tea for the police, and Lucy and John were sheltering in John's workshop.

But only Lucy and John actually witnessed the events on Effingham land. They did so from the loading bay where they stood looking across the valley for a sign of Dr. Appleby and Dr. Barber. They could see the dark shape of the dead insect close to the wall of one of Mrs. Effingham's upper fields, and above the wall, the roof of the police car with its blue light still flashing.

John could just make out the figures standing close to the corpse, but only Lucy, with the help of her field glasses, could identify them as her father and A.B. Two of the police were with them, but they appeared to be examining the sky rather than the insect at their feet.

Then, as if overtaken by the sudden need for shelter—whether from the rain or from a more deadly threat it was impossible to tell from this distance—all four figures hastened back to the gate leading into the field, and were then lost to view behind the wall.

Two fields below, there was more urgent activity, which Lucy followed closely through her glasses now that she could no longer see her father.

The movements of the horses and the humans in the big fields formed into a distant, silent ballet as the grooms tried to tempt the temperamental horses into surrender, and then lead them away one by one.

From all this activity, one figure detached itself. John could not identify it with his naked eye, but to Lucy there was no doubt that it was Mrs. Effingham. As her eyes followed the burly figure hastening across the field, she gave a running commentary to John.

"Yes, that's her, nearly at the gate. . . . Now she's opened it. She's running—yes, actually running now—toward her car. . . . Yes, I see, it's beginning to rain hard over there. And her horrible car's roof is down, as usual. Serves her right. It's getting soaked. She's starting to put up her roof. Now. . . oh, Lord!"

"What is it?" said John impatiently, and then saw, almost as he spoke, the reason for Lucy's exclamation. From the dark rain clouds above, an insect was falling fast, as fast as a small crashing plane, straight toward the Jensen and the large figure bending over the convertible's open roof.

Lucy could see through her glasses the white of Mrs. Effingham's face as she suddenly looked up, alarmed by the sound above her. There was a brief moment when nothing seemed to happen; then Mrs. Effingham must have recognized her imminent fate and at the same time made the decision to attempt a getaway. For suddenly the Jensen shot forward a split second before the black shape would have enveloped its driver.

Never had the power of that V8 engine been put to such critical use. The car's rear wheels threw up a cloud of spray from the newly wet road, and left the great insect splayed out on the ground behind it.

But its size in no way restricted the speed of its responses. In a second its wings were spread wide, and it was airborne again, flying fast above the road, ignoring easier game in the fields in its determination not to be foiled by its intended victim.

"John, John! Look what's happening." Lucy managed to exclaim, gripping her field glasses more closely to her eyes.

But John could see all right with his naked eyes, in spite of the light rain curtain across the valley. The road wound up the side of the fell with high stone walls on both sides, so that the mauve open car, with its driver winding the steering wheel from left to right and back again through the corners, momentarily disappeared and reappeared again a few hundred yards farther on.

From Gartholme, the landscape on the other side of the valley might have been the board of a dice game, the car and pursuer two contestants. At the start of a long straight bit of road, Mrs. Effingham threw a double six, and the power of her car gave her the advantage. But when she hit a series of sharp bends, it was the insect that seized the advantage, closing in on its prey and cutting the corners as it flew low in relentless pursuit.

The distance from Gartholme was increasing all the time, and the rain was falling more heavily. Only Lucy could follow the chase, and she was finding it difficult. She saw the Jensen disappear behind a spinney and the insect skim just above the trees on a shortcut course. She could just make out the shape of the car as it emerged, the insect closing the height as well as the distance. Then she lost pursued and pursuer behind rising ground, and was about to lower her glasses when she saw them again on the crest of a hill.

Car and insect were as one. In a brief flash of clarity, she saw the car stop as if it had hit a wall. There was a sudden confusion of spray and turmoil in which the car and attacker disappeared entirely, to reappear as an indeterminate dark shape a few yards farther along the road.

It was impossible to tell what had taken place, and Lucy waited tensely for the next occurrence.

"What's happened?" asked John.

"There's been a crash."

"Where's the insect?"

"I don't know," Lucy replied. Her eyes were aching with the concentration of peering through the lenses. A minute passed. The shape, like a dark bundle on the distant road, did not move. Then a squall cut down the visibility by half, and it was impossible to see even the far side of the valley. Horses, grooms, the police car, the Jensen, and the insect—all had gone. The curtain had come down at the end of the drama, concealing the stage set and the players alike. But no applause came from the audience of two huddled side by side in the barn. For them the real-life play had been too harrowing, and too many questions remained unanswered.

Instead, a fierce clap of thunder, the loudest they had yet heard, crashed overhead. The sky darkened, and the lights went on in the farm and in the cottages down the road. The rain poured down, as hard as it had on that morning Lucy had found the mysterious object in her orchard. What a long time ago that seemed now, that innocent, happy time before the insects had come to terrorize the village!

Scot was nuzzling up against their legs, and they both bent down to offer comfort. The noise was enough to strike fear in the least superstitious under everyday circumstances; but now, with death stalking the valley, it was impossible to disregard the proximity of the supernatural.

A spread of sheet lightning brought farm and cottages, the glistening road and bending trees and the rain itself, into sudden white illumination. It was an unusually prolonged flash, and when it cut off, the scene outside appeared darker than ever. Then Lucy saw that it was indeed darker, that the lights in the cottages and in Gartholme Farm were no longer shining out.

"The electricity's off," she said.

"It's caught one of the substations, or the cable's down," John said. "Makes the place look pretty dead."

Lucy realized how right this was as she stared out into the near darkness, and the storm raged louder and more fiercely than ever. She was more frightened than she had been bicycling up through the village in pursuit of John, even more frightened than the moment she saw the spread of legs and body and predatory head of the insect descending on her. Then she could do something. Now there was only worry—worry about her father and everyone else in the village, fear for Balliol locked up in his shed, fear for her own life.

The practical voice of John broke into Lucy's black thoughts. "This seems the right moment to switch on. I wanted to give the transformer a last check over, but it should be all right."

Lucy did not know what he was talking about until she saw him walk back into his workshop. There was a pause of several seconds, and then she heard a loud click. At once the lights in the farm came on again, not as bright as before and not quite steady either—but it was light where there had been darkness. To underline his success, John threw over another switch which cast a yellow gleam over the yard, illuminating the falling rain, the puddles and stream now running through it, the happy ducks and even the less happy hens crouched on the porch.

When it came to practical matters, John was a boy of few words. He came and stood beside Lucy at the loading bay, hands on his hips, looking out into the yard. "Well, it works," he said, not quite able to conceal the satisfaction in his voice.

It was still raining as hard as ever when the police car drove into the yard a few minutes later. It halted outside the barn, and the front passenger window was wound down. A face peered out and looked up. Lucy was thankful to see that it was her father.

"What are you doing here?" he demanded. "I left you at End House."

"We had to get the cows in," Lucy replied innocently. The rain made conversation difficult.

"Well, you come home with us now. I've had enough frights for one day."

The inspector got out of the driver's seat and stood in the rain, looking up at the two of them. "How is it you've got electricity here? The cable's down in the valley."

"Oh, we've got our own private supply," John called out, as if it was the most normal thing in the world. "Hydroelectricity, you know."

For Lucy, Millbeck was a better place. It was four o'clock, the storm was over, sunshine was shafting between the breaking clouds, and the fields and fells were sparkling as no other part of England can reflect the aftermath of rain. Two armed police had taken food and water to the pony and had reported him content. Lucy was making a mountain of scrambled eggs as they were all as hungry as Balliol, and she could hear the murmur of men's voices from the living room discussing the insect threat. There had been no more attacks since the storm had ceased. There would no doubt be more, but at least the menace was identified, and surely with all the resources of science and power behind them, these men would find a way of defeating the insects.

A woman had been killed on the other side of the beck, Lucy had heard the inspector report on the telephone. She had also overheard his report on Mrs. Effingham's accident.

"After the ambulance has picked up the body on the southwest road," the inspector had instructed his headquarters, "it should proceed on the upper road. In one mile the driver will observe the wreckage of a car in the ditch. It's lying on top of one of the insects—not a pretty sight. The driver was thrown out in the crash and fractured her skull against a tree. We've covered the corpse, and there's a soldier on duty nearby—in a roadmender's hut because we're not risking anyone outside if we can help it."

Lucy's mind was too stunned by too many violent and frightening events to take in fully the momentous truth that Mrs. Effingham would never again be tormenting the Thomsons, that the village had been relieved of one unpleasant burden it had been carrying for too long, and that the Jensen convertible, which had made the narrow lanes so dangerous, was a mass of twisted metal.

Perdition? Lucy did not wish that for her, or anyone, even though Mrs. Effingham had threatened Lucy herself with eternal damnation. All the same. . .

She carried the loaded tray into the living room. Besides the scrambled eggs, there was bread and butter and cake for the police inspector, his assistant, and the two scientists. And a pot of strong tea as Rachel had taught her to make it.

"A useful child you've got," commented the inspector, smiling at Lucy who privately thought she qualified for something more adult than "useful child" after the events of the day.

Dr. Barber launched into an account of his findings so far at the same time that he launched into his scrambled eggs. Wielding a fork, he said, "From my examination of the dead male and what's left of the female that died violently not far from it, I think we are dealing here with a member of the *Simuliidae* midge family. There are many hundreds of different kinds, and many have never been identified. They have something in common with the *Nigritarsis,* which is found in many damp parts of South Africa."

A.B. turned to Dr. Appleby. "When did you come back?"

Dr. Appleby told him, and A.B. exclaimed, "Ah —that's not a coincidence," with a note of triumph in his voice. "Just about the gestation period."

"What do you mean?" asked Lucy's father.

"I think you brought some *Simuliidae* eggs back with you—by mistake, I hasten to add."

Dr. Appleby was not convinced. "How? And anyway, not that size. They'd have to be as big as ten ostrich eggs to hatch out *those!*"

"Not necessarily. The growth could have been progressive, like common elephantiasis." He turned to Lucy. "Tell me again how big those

108

objects were that you and your friend found."

"About this long," said Lucy, holding her hands a yard apart.

"See what I mean? Those cast-off larva skins would normally produce an insect no longer than that. But the male was eight feet long by my measurements, and more than four feet thick, and the females are even bigger. Progressive overgrowth. If we ever find a pupa, it'll be even bigger than the larva shell, and at the final hatching—well, we've all seen. . ." And the entomologist applied himself more seriously to his food.

Later, Lucy considered that she had been right all along to prefer birds to insects when she heard of the complicated stages these *Simuliidae* and other families of midges and mosquitoes go through before they finally hatch. A.B. explained how the *corpus allatum* gland behind the insect's brain secretes the juvenile hormone at the larval stage, and that this controls its development until it undergoes metamorphosis into an adult.

"At some period," A.B. concluded, "these insects have experienced a massive hormone overdose—it might even have been absorbed at the egg stage. And yet you were in the desert," he said to Dr. Appleby. "That's the puzzling aspect. And you only brought back some succulents and sand. Succulents, dry desert, and sand don't add up to *Simuliidae,* or any other family of midge for that matter."

Dr. Appleby's mind went back to that night of the freak storm and to the sight of the desert the following morning. He remembered the near-magical bursting forth of a thousand grasses and plants from a desert that seemed as sterile as the surface of the moon, and the sudden appearance of insects that had later tortured them with their bites.

After a long pause, he said, "The desert wasn't as dry as all that, A.B. We hit it in freak conditions, and there was plenty of insect life where we were. In fact, I've only just stopped scratching my bites."

The inspector broke in here, "I know I'm just a layman in these things," he said, "but I can't see what the connection is between you getting bitten in the Kalahari desert and people being killed in Millbeck."

"That's what we've got to find out," said A.B. decisively.

Lucy could not resist quoting the entomologist's own aphorism: "The impossible may take a little longer."

Dr. Barber laughed and said, "Well done, my girl. But not much longer, I hope. Time presses, and these ghastly freaks can reproduce and spread all over the country." He turned to Dr. Appleby. "I'll take the plants with me, if you don't mind. And the spare sand you showed me."

"And you'll go in my car, with a motorcycle escort," said the inspector firmly as he got up. "You'll probably get stuck in the middle of the road again in your old metamorphosis of a tin-can machine."

Dr. Barber was halfway back to Manchester on the motorway, no doubt exceeding the speed limit by a wide margin, when Lucy's father raised the telephone. "I want an overseas call," Lucy heard him say. "Yes, a personal call, to Miss Mary Fleming at the University of Northern Cape Town. I don't have the number. She's a postgraduate student there. If you can't get her, put me through to police headquarters in Cape Town. This is a life and death matter."

Lucy turned to her father in amazement. "What do you want to talk to her for so suddenly?"

"It's just an idea. I've been going over every stage of our expedition. What we ate. What we could have picked up. It was not just by chance that that larva you found had emerged from the soil close to where I had planted the two aucurulas. I'm sure you were right when you said that it moved, as it would respond to the warmth of a hand. The larva was intact then—alive. The storm carried it away, along with others before or later, and they were swept down to the beck where they hatched as pupas, leaving some of the husks washed up on the bank."

The telephone rang, and Dr. Appleby picked it up. It was the call from Cape Town already. The switchboard operator at the university had sent out a message for Mary Fleming. A few seconds later, Dr. Appleby heard her familiar, happy, but also rather mystified, voice.

"We're having a little trouble here," began Dr. Appleby with what Lucy regarded as something of an understatement. "Trouble with the soil we dug out with the succulents. You remember we all sweated a great deal while we were digging—I remember my sweat pouring onto the aucurulas themselves as I tucked them into the bags. This is a long shot, but I was wondering if there was anything unusual in the bloodstream of any of us at that time. I was taking Silvasun against sunburn, some antimalaria pills earlier, and Piet and I were taking Entero-Viaform. This is a very personal question, but what were you taking?"

Lucy heard Mary Fleming laughing six thousand miles away but could not make out what she said. After a minute Dr. Appleby said, "That's very interesting. No, I won't waste any more of your time. You'll probably be reading in the *Cape Times* what is happening up here—they won't be able to keep it quiet much longer. Thank you very much."

Dr. Appleby sat staring across the room with a thoughtful expression on his face. Lucy did not want to interrupt his thinking, but at last she could not resist asking what was interesting.

"I think I mentioned to you that that nice, clever girl was on the plump side. Her complexion wasn't all that marvelous either, though I'd say better than it had been. It seems that for six months before we went on that expedition she had been taking a heavy course of hormone tablets to control her acne. That was the reason for her overweight condition, and she is now on thyroid pills to bring her weight back to normal.

"It's my belief that Mary Fleming's bloodstream

was carrying a high content of a hormone which was reflected—as it would be—in the makeup of her perspiration. I must have lost a pint of sweat working out there in the midday sun, so a great deal of this affected liquid must have fallen around the plants that Mary Fleming dug up, too. It's not impossible that midge eggs had been laid in that same sand—there have been stranger coincidences in nature."

Lucy broke in, laughing. "Daddy, you sound as if you're giving a lecture to your students."

Dr. Appleby did not laugh back. He was not cross at this comment, but he was deadly serious when he said, "If that's so, it's the most important lecture I've ever given."

Lucy said, "You mean when the midge eggs hatched out into larvae they absorbed some of the hormone which had already passed through a human body?"

"I mean just that. You know how small midges can be—a millimeter long or less. You don't need much additional hormone in the *corpus allatum* to upset the speed and degree of growth and metamorphosis in anything as small as that."

Lucy got up and looked out of the window across the fields. What a strange, precarious thing the cycle of nature is she was thinking. And what terrible responsibilities everybody carried for preventing disturbances like this, as well as for preserving endangered species, something that was much more widely discussed!

She remembered the golden eagles bravely mobbing that giant insect, knowing instinctively that it was unnatural and dangerous. And Balliol's fear of it. Dear Balliol—she could see the faint gray shape of his head looking disconsolately out of his shed in the dusk light. How he must be longing to walk about and graze!

They *must* somehow get rid of these terrible insects. But if guns were no good, then ... She turned to her father, who had got himself a glass of beer which he was sipping thoughtfully in the half light.

"Daddy, if hormones made that girl too fat and thyroid makes her thin again," she said, "why don't they give the midges a dose of thyroid?"

DEADLY DRAMA IN CUMBRIAN VALLEY

Several Deaths From Mysterious Insect Attacks

WHITEHAVEN, 5 September—A large area of west Cumbria has been placed under martial law by order of the Chief Constable of the County, and a statement from Emergency Military headquarters in Barrow states that all traffic movements in an area bounded by a line between Whitehaven, Buttermere, Hawkshead, and Broughton-in-Furness is subject to military control.

In a smaller area, defined below, inhabitants are

confined to their homes, and movements by military vehicles only are permitted.

Arrangements for the supply of food and other necessities are well in hand, the statement confirms.

The reason for these extraordinary measures is a localized plague of insects which attack humans as well as livestock, sometimes with fatal results. It is believed that the insects are unusually large, although reports that they are as big as birds have not been confirmed.

No reporting facilities of any kind for newspapers, sound broadcasting, or television, are at present being made available, the military authorities state. But they add that the measures are purely temporary and that every effort is being made to control the insects.

It is regretted that among those who have died as a result of the depredations of these noxious insects is that notable personality in the world of thorough-bred horse breeding, Mrs. Alice Effingham. Others who are believed to have died include. . .

From the *West Cumbrian Mail*

Britain's press was not used to being dealt with as high-handedly as the statement from military head-quarters suggested. With a nose for the truth that bromides like this only angrily stimulated, the newspaper and television reporters pressed relent-lessly to be allowed through the barrier at Brough-ton, and demanded a press conference and inter-view with the GOC troops enforcing martial law in Cumbria.

But the military authorities, under orders from the Home Office, refused all demands for inter-views and further information. For this reason, exaggerated stories stemming from rumor spread more alarm than an honest full statement would have done.

On the third day of martial law, three newsmen —one from an international agency, one from an American television network, and the third from a popular English tabloid newspaper—decided to take the law into their own hands.

They hired a helicopter, ostensibly to go to the Isle of Man, but when airborne persuaded the pilot with a £1,000 bribe in notes, to go north and fly low over the fells to the head of the Millbeck valley, and then down the length of it.

The helicopter was seen by a number of soldiers billeted in Millbeck village, and warning flares were shot in its direction. No insects had been seen all that day, but the presence of this large and unfamiliar intruder brought out a number of them from their places of concealment high up among the fells.

They attacked the helicopter without fear of its whirling blades, and although one of the insects was cut to pieces and stopped the engine, the weight of four more drove the helicopter down onto a rock with such force that it broke up on impact. No one survived the crash.

This disaster came as a warning to the military authorities, and to the Home Secretary as well as the press, and a more specific communiqué was issued that same evening, describing the size and nature of the insects. But this communiqué also quoted a statement from the president of the

Entomological Institute, Sir Rivers Bridges, that, regardless of size, midges and mosquitoes never strayed far from their breeding ground.

Unfortunately, the following day three cattle were killed while grazing in the valley next to Millbeck, some eight miles from the village. The news was suppressed by an emergency order from the Home Office.

The destruction of the helicopter and the evidence that the menace might spread farther afield, brought new urgency to the work in Dr. Austin Barber's laboratories at North Manchester University. It was understood by some of the entomologists that the absence of livestock—to say nothing of people—might drive the insects in desperation farther from their breeding ground. Others—but not Dr. Barber—disagreed.

This was not the only conflict that delayed the taking of effective countermeasures. The arrival of Sir Rivers Bridges, on Home Office instructions, to take over the research into means of destroying the insects, was another. In order to impress his own brilliance and importance on the well-known scientists—including Dr. Barber—already at work, he had ordered everybody to go back to the beginning and pursue his lines of inquiry.

Meanwhile, a sudden increase in numbers of insects suggested that a new generation had hatched, in spite of every effort to locate their breeding grounds among the remote tarns and bogs high up in the fells. Several more male corpses were discovered, and the remains were sent to Manchester for analysis.

These new young predators gave evidence of being less inhibited in their movements. On September 11, two insects were seen flying high over Cockermouth, outside the martial-law zone. A mobile light antiaircraft battery that was passing through the town on its way to Barrow got off a number of shots at the insects. After the first shot, they dropped like stones to ground level. It was concluded that it was these two that had been responsible for the death of a middle-aged farmer and his wife at a nearby farm.

It was decided to reactivate the air raid warning system, which had never been dismantled after the Second World War. From time to time, and with increasing frequency as the days passed, the wail of sirens sounded in one or another part of Cumbria as the ever increasing numbers of insects spread out on raids across the county, intent on the life-giving blood of cattle and sheep, and even dogs, as well as unfortunate or rash people who failed to hear the whine of the sirens or the deadly drone of the approaching insects.

By September 13 one hundred and twelve men, women, and children had succumbed to the menace. The tourist trade, which normally brought in so much wealth to the area, was dead. Farmers were carrying on in crippling circumstances with as much livestock as could be accommodated under cover, and making inroads into winter fodder stocks to keep them fed. Food distribution was under military escort only, many small industries had closed because of the difficulties of getting their work force to the factories, and all schools were closed.

The eyes of the world were focused on west Cumbria. Photographs of the giant insects had been published, as well as grotesque pictures of their victims, sprawled out over fell and field, road and farmyard. The term "buzzbug" had been coined early in the crisis, and it had been compared to the flying bomb "doodlebugs" of 1944–45, which had also killed so many innocent civilians.

One bright amateur statistician had calculated that, by September 14, the blood lost to the buzzbugs exceeded the needs of the hospital transfusion service for five years.

From the very first days, the critics were harrying the authorities for a solution. The campaign built up rapidly, encouraged by the absence of any firm information on progress. "Any reader might be forgiven for believing that the 'buzzbugs' can not only read, but have an intelligence service which might benefit from news of the countermeasures being taken against them," an editorial in *The Times* ironically opened.

On the same day, an entire family of father, mother, two teenage boys, and a five-year-old girl were all killed while bringing in their corn harvest north of Cockermouth. The following day, there was an explosion of wrath in every newspaper and on the television screens, and there was talk of the government falling.

119

On the morning of September 17, Lucy was looking out of the window of End House down the valley, waiting for the arrival of the vehicle which daily brought a group of children to the house for lessons. School had long since closed, and Dr. Appleby, who had made only two journeys to Manchester since the crisis, owing to the difficulties of the journey, had volunteered to give the Millbeck children of Lucy's age daily lessons. "At least you're going to be hot stuff on the botany questions at exam time," Dr. Appleby had commented one morning.

Lucy noticed that there was an unusual level of traffic on the village road that morning. Khaki-colored trucks packed with troops followed one another at close intervals. One of them halted down the road beside the gate leading into Balliol's field, and a dozen soldiers jumped down, rapidly spreading out across the grass. Dr. Appleby was peering over Lucy's shoulder, as interested as she was in what was happening.

"What are they doing in our field?" asked Lucy. She could see Balliol pacing restlessly up and down his hut. He seemed to be as indignant at this intrusion as Lucy.

"They look businesslike enough," commented Dr. Appleby.

"They've all got guns," said Lucy. "Look, small guns."

"Those are called Capchur rifles," her father told

her. "I've seen them in the mammal labs at Manchester. They're like shotguns, but they're not for killing. They're for darting. They're charged with carbon dioxide and usually fire a dart for putting animals out temporarily. I suppose they're mounting a major attack on the buzzbugs."

Lucy stared at her father in astonishment. "But I thought we wanted to kill them—not put them out temporarily?"

"Let's just wait and see."

And that is just what they did.

Hundreds of soldiers, all armed with Capchur rifles, fanned out across the entire length and breadth of the Millbeck valley. They wore flak jackets as some sort of protection, and settled themselves close to stone walls or under trees in groups of three.

Later in the morning, numbers of cattle trucks followed the personnel carriers up the road, depositing sheep and cattle in great numbers in all the fields.

The rest of the village followed the events of that morning with equal fascination. Few of them recognized the nature of the army's weapons. To the unfortunate people of Millbeck, most of whom had not left their homes for more than two weeks, and were frustrated and bored and angry, as well as frightened, it looked as if full-scale warfare was about to break out.

John Thomson, one of the less bored and frustrated people, had been waiting in his workshop for the arrival of the morning army vehicle to take him down to End House. After giving sterling service during the great storm, his hydroelectric service had broken down four days later, and he had been trying to get permission to follow the line of the cable down to the beck, with military escort, to trace the fault. So far, he had failed.

He could now see a number of khaki-clad figures moving across the fields to the beck where his dam and turbine and generator were situated, and he hoped that there would be no interference with his scheme.

When he saw a strange herd of cattle being taken from a truck and driven into their big field, he felt as indignant at this act of trespass as Lucy had been. But, like few other villagers, he recognized the nature of the plan. It was clear to him that today a major attack on the buzzbugs was to be mounted, and he watched for the outcome with fascinated interest.

Back at End House, Dr. Barber had arrived, looking gaunt and haggard from worry and lack of sleep. "Do you mind if I watch the show from here?" he asked. "It seems right somehow."

Dr. Appleby welcomed him in and asked him what he meant.

A.B. turned to Lucy in answering this question. "Well, love, you were the first to spot them, and no one believed you—not until you told your dad— and that's bad considering what a birdwatcher you are. So it seems right somehow that we should all watch the end of them together."

"Do you really think so?" asked Lucy. "Are you going to kill them all today?"

"Kill them or something like it," replied A.B. enigmatically, indicating the scene outside the window. Every field in sight was filled with livestock, live bait where for days there had been no prey for the buzzbugs. Crouched in groups of three around the perimeter of the fields were men of the Lancashire Yeomanry in camouflaged field uniform, guns at the ready.

"Every alloy slug in every gun is loaded with a compound of chemical concentrate," said A.B. with satisfaction. "Now all we've got to do is wait."

The whole village of Millbeck, the inhabitants, military, and police, waited tensely for more than two hours on that gray September morning. Even among those who still did not understand the nature of the operation, there was a feeling that today marked the culmination of their ordeal. Either the buzzbugs would at last be defeated, or, if that failed, everybody would be evacuated from the valley, perhaps never to return. And then, who could tell what control over the whole nation the deadly insects might later achieve?

Just before eleven o'clock, with a light drizzle falling and visibility reduced to less than a mile, the first faint deep drone was heard at the far end of the village. A few seconds later, the familiar outline of an insect appeared, flying fast just below the base of the clouds on a southerly course.

From the air, Millbeck presented a very different sight in contrast with the past days, when nothing seemed to move in the valley except objects along the roads which were unappetizing for buzzbugs. Now the fields were again full of rich game. Without hesitation, the insect dropped fast toward a herd of cattle innocently grazing the rich grass of David Howe's best field.

The familiar plunging attack followed. As the victim lay prostrate and helpless beneath the weight of the insect, a muted explosion, no louder than the bursting of a blown-up paper bag, sounded out, and was repeated by others. A dozen darts, fired from every direction, pierced the hairy, black, barrellike body of the insect. It appeared to be only slightly put out by this assault, pausing momentarily in its hungry drawing of blood from the neck of the cow, but not bothering to withdraw its proboscis.

Then it lifted off from the dying animal and took to the air again, flying as swiftly and determinedly as ever, in search of new victims.

More attacks followed, at increasing frequency, until as many as twenty buzzbugs were at their deadly business at once. John watched an attack in their big field. It took place at the same spot where Madge had nearly succumbed. Rachel Deering watched an attack on the fell slope behind her cottage from a back window and thought she was dreaming. Sam Dodgson, on the other hand, was unimpressed.

Down at End House, the mass attack was watched with the greatest anxiety. There was a good view over a wide area from the living room windows, and Lucy's field glasses were in great demand. At one time, no fewer than five of the imported livestock were suffering fatal attack, and Lucy hid her eyes, no longer able to bear seeing the suffering.

Dr. Appleby put his arm around her shoulders. "Don't watch, love. But remember that they would all have gone to the abattoir in the end anyway to feed this meat-eating nation. And this business has got to be ended."

"But, it's not working. It's a waste of lives."

A.B., hearing this comment, called from another window: "Cheer up! It may take an hour or two to have any effect."

Lucy kept her eyes closed, listening to the sinister plop-plop. . .plop-plop-plop of the gas guns.

Colonel Robert "Bobby" Samson, commanding the first battalion of the Lancashire Yeomanry, breasted the summit of Eskdale Hause, sat down on a rock, and started to fill his pipe. With him were his adjutant, a very young second lieutenant, and six troopers. It was a bright autumn day, crisp and clear—so clear that you could just make out the low, dark shape of the Isle of Man, Snaefell rising abruptly in the center on the western horizon.

Colonel Samson loved the Lakeland mountains and had enjoyed leading his small party all day over the fells above Millbeck. As to the outcome of this final reconnaissance, he had mixed feelings. For two days his men had roamed the fells of west Cumbria in search of buzzbugs, dead or alive. Last night his second-in-command reported to his headquarters in Rangarth that nothing had been found. Not a trace.

Intelligence had revealed that there had been eighty-five insect attacks in the Millbeck valley on September 17. His men claimed that not one had got away without receiving at least one dart, and most had been hit a dozen times.

Colonel Samson struck a match and, cupping it in his hands, sucked the flames onto his pipe. Richly scented tobacco smoke drifted away on the wind.

"Gentlemen," said the colonel. "We're soldiers. We don't pretend to understand science. But we've carried out our orders. We hit those damn insects square in the middle where it hurts, and it seems to have done the trick. Speaking as a soldier, I'd have preferred live ammunition and blown them to bits. Good target practice. But those darts have driven them off, all right."

The colonel surveyed the magnificent panorama of mountains, all covered with a subtle blend of rock and grass, bracken and heather, and decided he would take his next leave up here now that it was open to tourists again.

Then he turned to his officers and men, sucking

on his pipe with satisfaction. "Gentlemen, I think we can say we've beaten this damn bug. Good show." And he got up from the rock and began to lead his men down the long, steep, rocky track into the valley.

On the same afternoon, Lucy and John were up on the slopes of Craig Fell, five miles from Colonel Samson and two thousand feet lower in altitude. They were in the same place from which Lucy had seen first the golden eagles, and then that awful dark shape in the sky—a shape that was already a nightmare memory in her mind.

On the previous evening, martial law had ceased over west Cumbria, and all restrictions had been lifted. The village had been full of parties to celebrate its liberation, and many toasts were drunk to the Lancashire Yeomanry for their work in ridding Millbeck of the terror of the buzzbug. On the following day, Dr. Barber would be returning to Manchester, and soon school would reopen.

"Before we go back to prison," said Lucy to John, "come and see if my eagles are all right. You bike, I'll ride. O.K.?"

John said he would like that. He had got his hydroelectricity going again in the morning—it was only a minor fault—and he did not have much else on his mind.

So they lay in the bracken, eyes glued to the dark rock face of Cairngale opposite, glancing occasionally at the clear sky above. John did not possess

Lucy's patience, and was amazed how she could remain absolutely still for so long, moving only her head and arms slowly as she swiveled her field glasses.

After a long while, Lucy said softly, "It's too good to be true."

"What?" asked John, but realizing as he spoke what Lucy must mean. He examined every lodge, every crevice, with infinite care but to no effect.

"They're alive," whispered Lucy. "The brave, lovely things, they're alive. I'll bet they chased away those filthy bugs just as they did the first time. Look," and she passed John the field glasses and directed him where to look.

For a long time John could not identify the birds against the dark rock, and he had almost given up when he caught a glimpse of a flash of movement. He managed to follow it until it was against the lighter tone of a scree slope. "But they're huge!" he exclaimed. Even he could see how much bigger they were than the buzzards Lucy had often pointed out to him.

"And beautiful," sighed Lucy. "Watch them come out against the sky now."

She was right. First one, then the second eagle flew higher so that the great breadth and depth of the wings were shown off. As they turned, soaring higher above the fells, John could see how dark they were, and how long their tails, compared with buzzards.

He passed the glasses back to Lucy, and as she put them to her eyes, an ornithologist's miracle occurred across the valley. As the great birds soared higher, two smaller birds came into view, wings beating with less grace but determinedly, as they seemed to attempt to gain equal height with the bigger birds.

It was not until the sun caught the undersurface of the wings of this second pair of birds that Lucy dared to believe her excited suspicions were true. They were the young golden eagles, so recently chicks on some unknown ledge on that face of rock, and now fledglings, perhaps taking to the air for the first time, with the parents hovering protectively above. There was no doubt about it. Both her books on British birds of prey told of the heavy white streaking that often extends almost for the length of the wing of immature golden eagles. If they were not flying for the first time, then surely she, Lucy Appleby, member of the National Society for the Protection of Birds, had made the first sighting!

When Lucy said, "Those are fledges—see?" it sounded almost banal. But John caught the note of excitement in her voice. For Lucy this was as great a moment as the moment had been when the lights glowed at Gartholme. Both were triumphs in a late summer that had known so much fear and tragedy.

For John, this had suddenly become more than a moment of triumph. It had become a moment of truth, too. The sight of the eagles signified for John that the time had come to make his confession about Mrs. Effingham's padlock to Lucy.

She was as sensible as he guessed she would be.

"You bury that conscience of yours, John Thomson," she said. "First of all, you didn't do it. Second, even if you had, you would probably have got off for what I think they call 'extreme provocation.' Third, no one will ever know whether you might not have stopped yourself at the last second. Knowing you, you probably would have stopped."

They were almost back at the stone fold where Balliol and Scot awaited them when John paused to scratch his ankle under his jeans. "Did I get *bitten* up there!" he exclaimed. "You bird watchers must have skins like hide."

"No we haven't," Lucy replied feelingly. "You're not the only one. It's all that lying about in the bracken." And she scratched the back of her neck until it hurt.

At End House, Dr. Barber was anxious to leave and return to Manchester, especially as the lights on his old banger were like candles in a hurricane. He was also anxious to say good-bye to Lucy, for a very special reason.

When she did come in through the front door, with John behind her, a great deal of Balliol's gray coat sticking to her jeans, and her cheeks still flushed with triumph, the entomologist had to listen to the account of her sighting, and to share the excitement which they all felt. Fledgling golden eagles not five miles away! What an aerial contrast with the buzzbugs which had terrorized them for so long!

Dr. Appleby said, "A.B.'s going back to base now, Lucy. But I think he's got something to say to you first."

Lucy turned to him, wondering what she had done wrong. But his face, though still showing tiredness after his ordeal, was set in the old puckish smile. "You know about the impossible," he began enigmatically. "Well, it did take longer. But it would have taken longer still—and maybe too long —if it hadn't been for you."

"What do you mean?" asked Lucy, sitting down with surprise.

"It was something you said to your dad—and he passed it on to me more as a joke than anything else. About thyroids. You said, 'Why don't they give them a dose?' And that's just what we did."

Dr. Barber told them about the struggle at the entomological laboratories in Manchester, how he and his assistants had worked alone and at night after the official team of scientists under Sir Rivers Bridges had gone to bed, and had come up with a formula which had contained a high proportion of sheep's thyroid gland and the same poison used in Mylodol.

"It was a double-banked weapon—and a triple-banked risk," A.B. continued with a grin. "But the other team had nothing. And we at least had a kill-or-cure remedy—if the thyroid didn't counter the results of excessive hormone intake, the poison would kill them. That was the reasoning, and the Home Office accepted it for the lack of anything better. So, with a drug company working around the clock, we had five thousand alloy buzzbug darts ready by the morning of the sixteenth. And you know the rest of the story."

There was a long silence in the living room at End House. Then Dr. Appleby said, "Oh no, we don't, A.B. You haven't tied up the last knot in your plot. Which worked, the poison or the thyroid?"

"I wish I could tell you. It was an imperfect experiment because no one knows. Never will, I suppose. They may have assumed the millimeter size nature intended them to be—nice, ordinary *Simuliidae* that nip and leave irritation and a red mark. Or they've gone away somewhere to die, like elephants. All we know is that they're not here any more," Dr. Barber ended with triumphant satisfaction.

At the same time, John bent down and scratched furiously, pulling up his jeans. They all saw a number of red marks around his ankle. "What do you mean, they're not here any more?" he asked complainingly.

Dr. Barber leaned down, examining the evidence, and laughed heartily. "Very interesting," he said. "But at least, now that they're back to their proper size, they've left you some blood."

He stood up and made for the door. "Goodbye," he said to them all. "It's time for me to bang my way home in my sturdy automobile. 'The possible we can do today,' eh, Lucy love?"

"This time I hope the impossible doesn't take

longer," Lucy replied, studying the ancient Hillman doubtfully. "Good luck."

It was a beautiful, still, late afternoon, with the sun slanting across the valley, and Balliol grazing peacefully in his field. They all still felt the wonderful relief from the absence of fear, and there was complete silence in the village—until, with a mighty roar, A.B.'s car burst into raucous life, and then backfired its way down the hill like an armored car with its 40mm. gun in action.

BRUCE CARTER, the well-known British author of numerous books for young people and adults, was born and lives in England. He wrote his first book for children twenty-five years ago—*The Perilous Descent*—which is still in print, and is in the same tradition of science fiction as *Buzzbugs*. Bruce Carter is married to the children's writer and artist Charlotte Hough, and they both enjoy traveling to obscure parts of the world where they photograph and write about rich wildlife.